SKYLA GRAY

The Revenant's Heart

Monster Research Facility #2

Contents

Chapter One

The snake coils on my desk, poised to strike. I'm admiring the lovely curve of its fangs when the call arrives. I glance at my phone, my hands perfectly still where they hold the needle and thread that are stitching up the reptile's scaled belly. *Ash Valley, Arizona*, the screen announces.

I've never heard of the place, and I'm not in the habit of answering phone calls of unknown origin. So after a moment, I return to my delicate work. I finish sewing the snake skin over the inner wire, snip off the extra thread, and carefully place the glass eyeballs into its head to finish the illusion of life. When light strikes its yellow eyes, I can almost picture the sinuous twist of scales against my desk, the dry rattle of its tail.

As I sit back to search for flaws in my work, my phone buzzes again.

I stretch my fingers, push my glasses up my nose, and sigh. Even though I stubbornly keep my gaze on my project, my focus is lost. The real world has already invaded, and my concentration is broken, along with my peace. Worse, a glance at the screen tells me it's voicemail this time.

I push the snake back on the table, among the dozens of other small creatures I've lovingly reconstructed over the past week.

I adore my little collection of critters, though I don't feel the same spark as I do with my *other* creations. The cat with antlers mounted above my television, the rabbit with raven's feathers that watches over me when I sleep—those are my favorites, the ones that bring me the greatest joy.

But I haven't felt inspired to create lately. I can barely manage the drive to finish these reconstructions, let alone one of my beautiful amalgamations.

The thought stamps out any joy I gained from finishing my project. That, plus another insistent buzz from my phone. I don't want to look. I'm terrified by the idea that it could be one of my former classmates reaching out with faux concern. Or someone from the University of Southern California calling for another *wellness check* that oozes of condescension. There is no one in the world I want to talk to right now. But if I don't listen to that voicemail, it will itch in the back of my skull all day.

And I already have enough on my mind to torture myself with. Spending all this time aimlessly in my apartment means that I'm familiar with being alone with my thoughts, and they are not pleasant company. When I think of all the empty hours stretched out ahead of me, I feel sick with dread.

As hard as I've been trying over these past few weeks, I haven't found a way to reignite that vital spark I once had inside of me, pushing me onward. I just feel...empty. Not even the things I usually love, like my taxidermy, can bring back that piece of me that's gone missing.

Because as much as I love my hobbies, I've never been a person who's very good at filling the empty hours with them. I'm at my best when I'm learning and working. Not sitting around in my apartment like this.

Again and again, my mind returns to that mysterious voice-mail waiting for me.

It can't be anything good, I keep telling myself. But I have to know. And it's going to be impossible for me to focus until I do. With a sigh, I pull off my gloves, let my sheet of red hair tumble out of its tight ponytail, and pick up my phone. As I press it to my ear, I'm already bracing myself for some new disappointment or pain.

A woman's unfamiliar voice speaks in my ear.

"My name is Dr. Calliope Wright. I'm calling about a unique job opportunity in Ash Valley, Arizona, relevant to your field of study. I'm fully aware of your parting from USC's program and am prepared nonetheless to offer you a position here at the Melsbach Research Facility. Please call back for more details."

I slowly lower the phone from my ear, frowning. The details were sparse—very sparse—but the message left no room for misinterpretation. A job opportunity. Even though she knows I dropped out. It seems too good to be true.

But really, what choice do I have? I owe it to myself to at least call back and get more information. I do it right away, before I can lose my nerve. The line rings once, twice, and someone picks up.

"Dr. Wright."

I push to my feet and begin to pace my tiny apartment to work off my nerves. "Hello, this is Lucy Sullivan, returning your message about a job opportunity."

"Ms. Sullivan, yes. I'm delighted to hear from you. I know my message was vague."

I make a noncommittal noise, waiting for her to continue.

"I'm afraid I'm limited in how much I can say over the phone. The nature of my work is...unusual, and highly secretive. I cannot give many details unless you come and sign an NDA in person, but I'd be delighted to offer you a complimentary flight and stay in town while you get a better sense of what you're signing up for."

My brow furrows. I'm silent for a moment as I process that. "I'm not even in the state," I say, letting the doubt seep into my tone. *And a med school dropout,* I add silently.

"I'm aware, Ms. Sullivan. But as I understand it, you have little else but free time right now, yes?"

I bite my lip and glance around my empty apartment at my various taxidermy projects. "Yes. You mentioned you were aware of—" I clear my throat. "I quit the program."

"Indeed, and it was a shame, in my opinion. I believe that USC's loss can be our gain. We do not care about degrees here, Lucy. We only care that you are talented, open-minded, and curious. The rest you can learn."

There's a fragile flicker of hope inside of me. But I dig my nails into my palm, trying to stifle it. Something's off. What kind of a place would offer a job after I dropped out? And why does she speak like she already knows me? "A typical interview would involve you asking questions, not selling me the job," I say slowly.

"This is not an interview, and there is nothing typical about the MRF," Dr. Wright says. "We've already done our research on you. We only reach out to candidates who we believe would be a good fit for our facility. In lieu of a formal interview, we prefer to have candidates come in person so we can evaluate their response to the unique nature of our research."

There are several red flags here. Yet instead of putting me off, that only seems to make my curiosity surge. It's getting harder to tamp down the little voice that whispers *what if?*

"Can you tell me anything more about the position?" I ask, trying to remain level-headed. "It's a research facility, I believe you mentioned?"

"Indeed, it is. Though your position will be that of a hands-on practitioner."

I rub a temple, trying—and failing—to make sense of that. "Is this a government facility?"

"We're privately funded."

Finally, a straight answer, which makes me probe further. "And the nature of your research is...?"

"Classified, I'm afraid. I know this is all very strange, but I truly cannot give many details over the phone. More will be explained if you come to visit us in person, but—"

"Will I be helping people?" I blurt out, interrupting her before she can continue her practiced nonanswer. That's what I really want to know. That's what matters.

There's a pause. And then Dr. Wright says, almost gently, "You will be helping patients in dire need of an open mind and a kind hand, Ms. Sullivan, I can promise you that."

It's hardly an answer. I should be suspicious that she's giving me so little information. And yet...she's already told me exactly what I need to hear. Enough that my curiosity demands I go take a look at whatever they're offering, at least.

Plus, it's not as though I have anything better to do.

I take a deep breath and nod to myself before I say out loud, "How soon can you fly me out?"

Chapter Two

Next thing I know, I'm stepping off a plane, jittery with nerves. I'm usually not a nervous flyer, but my anxiety about arriving in Ash Valley kept me on the edge of my seat the whole trip here.

It all feels surreal. I still hardly know anything about this place or the job I'm being offered. The internet held very little information about this small town in the Sonoran Desert, and no information about the place I'm potentially working at, the Melsbach Research Facility. The whole thing is very strange indeed. Yet every time I balked at the idea of going through with this, I thought of Dr. Wright's promise that I could help people and those long, empty hours in my apartment with nothing but taxidermy in my future.

I stare out the window of the cab as it takes me to my hotel. This is a quaint little desert town nestled in a valley, as its name suggests. I see more saguaro than people on the drive, which is a stark contrast to the busy city streets and smog of Los Angeles. We pass by stout adobe houses, family-owned businesses with hand-painted signs, and tiny neighborhoods bursting with color and personality. No copy-paste identical homes or overly modern chain businesses to be seen. The whole place has a timeless feel; it's hard not to find it charming.

And it's quiet. That's what strikes me most of all. It's soothing to not be surrounded by the constant busyness and noise of the city.

"So what brings you to Ash Valley?" the cab driver asks, glancing at me in the rearview mirror.

"A job interview," I say, which seems simpler than explaining that a woman called me and issued me a personal offer based on reasons I still don't understand.

The man's brow furrows as if my answer is strange. I realize, belatedly, it probably is. This doesn't seem like a place bursting with job opportunities, especially not for people flying in from out of town.

"Interview?" he repeats. "But where... Oh." He stops, eyes widening with realization, and his gaze shifts from the mirror to the road. "Never mind."

It's an odd response. But honestly, I'm too tired from the flight and generally skeptical about small talk to put any more effort into the conversation, so I'm content to sit with my hands on my lap and stare out the window for the rest of the ride. He doesn't say another word. In fact, he barely looks me in the eye, even when he helps me with my bag as he drops me off.

* * *

After seeing the rest of the town, I'm not surprised to find that I'll be staying in a sweet little bed-and-breakfast rather than a chain motel. It's as delightful as expected, with its southwestern design and colorful garden of succulents. The owner herself meets me out front and takes me to my room, chattering excitedly all the while in a way that tells me she doesn't often get out-of-towners staying here.

"Ms. Wright has arranged everything for you," she tells me. "A car will be here in the morning to take you to the *Facility*." She places an almost reverent emphasis on the last word. "Since a lot of the locals are a little, well, *you know*." She shoots me a meaningful look over her shoulder.

"I don't, ac—" I start.

"There have been rumors about that place over the years, of course, but I'm not one to judge," she continues without pause. "What goes on there ain't none of my business, as far as I'm concerned. Ah! Here we are." She stops in front of a doorway and turns to beam at me. "Just let me know if you need anything."

Once I shut the door behind me, I breathe a sigh of relief. Managing small talk with strangers is certainly something I'll have to get accustomed to if I end up settling in here. The room itself is a sweet little accommodation, with stucco walls and paintings of desert landscapes and cattle. It would be cheesy if it wasn't so charming.

Still, it can't quite shake the lingering unease of the locals' words. Maybe I should be intimidated by this—the strange phone call out of the blue, the way they talk about *the Facility* like it's some kind of mythical creature. But I've always had a taste for the strange and unique, and I can't deny that it gives me a thrill.

I carefully lay out my outfit for the morning on the bed: a crisp white blouse and a black pencil skirt. I smooth out imaginary wrinkles and practice the answers for common interview questions under my breath until I'm tired enough to sleep.

* * *

After experiencing the small-town charm of the rest of Ash Valley, I can see why the locals might have their reservations about the Melsbach Research Facility, even from a glance. The place is huge and imposing, and its boxy utilitarian design sticks out like a sore thumb in comparison to the rest of the town's design. Even situated on the edge of Ash Valley, it is a glaring mark of *other* lurking on the horizon.

"I promise it's not as intimidating on the inside," my driver says. He's a reedy man a few years younger than me who introduced himself as Ezra and thankfully seemed to infer I wasn't interested in further small talk.

I could probably get more information from him if I tried, but nerves make my mouth go dry. By the time we pull through the gates, my excitement has curdled into anxiety. It was all very mysterious and curiosity-piquing right up until I saw that the place looked like some sort of secret government lab. I don't care how curious I am or how lucrative it is, but if this place has something to do with weapons manufacturing or anything of that ilk, I'll be out in a moment. My goal has always been to help people, and nothing will be able to tempt me into doing harm instead.

As we walk in the door, a security guard waves us through a metal detector and issues me a temporary ID card. The lobby inside is all metal and blank walls, giving no further information about what goes on in this place. There are a few tables and armchairs clustered around a coffee station, perhaps in an effort to make it more welcoming. But it's not working, especially given the eerie emptiness, and the fact that there's no actual coffee.

"Hm," Ezra says, glancing around the room with a furrowed brow. Perhaps the emptiness is unusual, then. "Dr. Wright was supposed to meet you here, but—"

"Ezra!" A woman, very pale beneath her freckles, peeks through the door across the room before hurrying over. "Thank God. We need you. X-15 is—"

"This is Lucy Sullivan, a new potential hire," Ezra interrupts with forced cheer.

She blanches even further—her complexion turning almost greenish—and spares me barely a glance before looking back at Ezra. "It's urgent," she says.

"Understood." Ezra looks at me. "I'm sorry, but—"

"Emergencies can't be helped," I say, though I'm *dying* of curiosity. "Go on."

He flashes me a grateful smile and walks away with the flustered woman, who is vibrating with stress at this point.

That leaves me alone in the front lobby, unsure about what to do with myself. After a moment—and an awkward exchange of glances with the security guard—I sit on an armchair and smooth my skirt down.

I sit there for five minutes. Ten. Twenty. At that point, I start to wonder if perhaps this is a practical joke after all. Even if it isn't, is a company this disorganized one I want to work for?

Still, what can I do? Walk out without my ride?

Finally, the door bursts open and another woman carrying a folder under one arm appears. She has dark hair cut in a shoulder-length bob. I assumed I'd be one of the youngest people working here as a twenty-seven-year-old who didn't quite finish med school, but she seems even younger than me. It makes me wonder what kind of clandestine research facility makes a habit of recruiting employees in their twenties.

"Hi, thanks so much for waiting," she says. Her smile is warm, genuine. "We appreciate the patience. I'm Mara Vance, and I'm here to give you the basics of the position you're being offered."

She extends her hand. I hesitate, considering telling her that I've changed my mind and I'd like to leave. But then I imagine walking out that door and having to wonder for the rest of my life what was behind that metal door.

"Lucy Sullivan," I say, shaking her hand.

"Nice to meet you." She leads me to the door, scans both of our IDs, and we walk into an empty white hallway. "I saw in your file that you've already signed the NDA. Freaky, I know. I'm going to show you around a bit and introduce you to the subject that you'll be treating if you accept the offer to work here."

Subject. The word sinks into my brain and sends a thrill through me, but I'm trying not to get ahead of myself. "I was under the impression I'd be meeting with Dr. Wright." We turn at the end of the hall and are faced with *another* blank white hallway marked only by metal doors. There's an eerie emptiness to this place, a stark lack of personalization that seems like it would make it all too easy to get lost in the maze of hallways. Each one might as well have been copied and pasted. I imagine an endless maze of these identical hallways within the building, and it makes me dizzy.

"Yes, well, we have a bit of a situation," Mara says, wincing. "Things are a little, um, well"—she tucks a strand of hair behind her ear, a nervous gesture, as she seems to search for the words—"*lively*, lately. We had some large-scale layoffs and a big revamp of our policies. Everyone's working hard to pick up the slack, and we're recruiting plenty of new hires lately, but it's still all..." She waves her hand.

That's all...frustratingly vague, but I have the distinct impression that Mara isn't sure how much she's allowed to say. Another red flag. This place seems disorganized, unpredictable. But...my God, I have never been so curious, so I'm certainly not planning on walking away until I at least get a glimpse of what this job will be.

Mara leads me to a door the same as all of the other doors, except for a small metal sign designating it as X-14. She instructs me to swipe my keycard, and just as I do, there's a loud thump from behind the door beside mine, like something slammed against it *hard*. Considering how quiet it is, the rooms must be soundproofed, so I cannot imagine how loud whatever that was must've been for us to hear it.

We both stare in that direction. I notice that sign reads X-15, the same designation mentioned by the girl who snatched Ezra away for some type of emergency.

"Let's, um... I'm sure it's fine!" Mara squeaks out, and rushes into the room, leaving me no choice but to follow.

The room we enter is small and boxy, holding a metal desk, a single chair, and a control panel with an array of buttons and switches. The desk is facing what appears to be an observation window looking into the next room, though it's currently shuttered.

"So—" Mara takes the folder out from beneath her arm and scans it. "Right. If you accept the offer, you'll be working with Subject X-14, the—" She stops whatever she was about to say, as if realizing something. She clears her throat, reads the file, and her eyes widen.

"And that *work* would consist of what, exactly?" I prompt.

I was promised details during this visit, and it's beginning to grate on me that I haven't received them yet. I want to know why she's referring to him as a *subject* rather than a *patient*. "Dr. Wright told me it was hands-on work rather than research."

Mara shuts the file and looks up at me. "Right. Yes. Sorry, this isn't usually my job. You'll be acting as a general practitioner, essentially, tending to the subject's physical needs. His...condition...is unique, so your treatment will likely be experimental in nature." Her fingers tap against her arm, betraying nerves.

I open my mouth to ask another question, but before I can, she continues. "As I mentioned, we've had a change in staffing and are going through a number of significant policy overhauls, and that includes updating our files on the subject. But I'd be remiss not to mention that Subject X-14 has a history of violence. But it's—I'm not saying you shouldn't be careful, but..." she stutters. I get the feeling she's going off-script with this, and it's probably information she's not exactly *supposed* to tell me. "He wasn't treated well before. He has considerable medical trauma. I hope you won't judge him too harshly based on your immediate impression. That's all I'm going to say."

I stare at her for a moment, unsure what exactly to say to that. Finally, I settle on, "I understand." A pause, and then I venture, "So I take it this man, my patient"—it feels too odd to call him a subject—"is some kind of criminal?" He must be if he's locked up here. As I wonder what kind of people could possibly require an environment like this, I have to suppress a shiver.

Mara hesitates. "Well...it's a bit more complicated than that," she says, with a flicker of a smile. "I think it's best if I just show you. Are you ready?"

I take a breath, anticipation rippling through me. The truth is that I have no idea if I'm ready because no one has really given me any indication of what to expect. But my curiosity refuses to be ignored any longer. "Of course."

She reaches over to adjust a lever, and the metal shutters on the observation window begin to open. I look into the adjacent room, and my eyes land on the man I'll be treating for the first time.

But he isn't really a man at all. He is something else entirely.

Chapter Three

The subject—the word fits now—leans against the wall, eyes shut and tattooed arms folded over his broad chest. He's dressed in baggy orange clothing like a prisoner would wear. He is exceptionally tall, long and lean, an imposing figure even with his slouched posture and lowered head. A mop of dark hair shadows his face, long on top and shaved shorter on the sides. His silhouette is that of a normal man, but upon a closer look, it's impossible to mistake him for that.

He is a collection of beautiful parts thrown haphazardly together. There's a shocking lack of care in how the pieces have been arranged. Lines of stitches and metal staples crisscross his body, piecing together sections of flesh that are impossibly *green* in hue.

A medley of tattoos crawling over his arms and neck adds to the chaotic effect, and silver piercings mark one eyebrow and the side of his nose. When he opens his eyes, his left eye is a pale blue, the right a deep, dark brown. One corner of his mouth is torn open, the skin pulled upward by poor stitching across his cheek, revealing a sliver of teeth and freezing his face in a permanent lopsided snarl. When he looks toward the window, as if sensing us there, his expression shifts and it looks more like a smirk.

His left hand is missing from the wrist down, leaving only a bandaged stump. His right leg juts out crookedly, bent at a strange angle that shouldn't be possible for him to stand on. There's a slipshod brutality to his design. He was given far less care and attention than I give to my own taxidermy creations, made by cruel hands for a purpose I can only imagine to be violent. The effect should be alarming, disturbing. And it is. Yet, still...

He's beautiful.

I realize I'm leaning forward, gripping the edge of the metal desk so hard, it hurts. Mara is looking at me. I take a deep breath and force myself to relax, lean back, as if I'm not salivating over the idea of learning more about this... this *creature*.

"Fascinating," I say, hoping that will convey my interest without making me seem like a madwoman. Am I supposed to be frightened of him? I am, but curiosity overtakes it.

Mara's lips quirk into a smile. "Do you have any questions?"

I have plenty. But I've always been the type of person who prefers to answer her own questions. I don't want Mara to explain the nature of this man—monster?—to me; I want to get in there and figure it out myself. "Should I call him X-14 or something else?"

"The file indicates that his name is Victor."

"Victor," I repeat, and frown. "Like Victor Frankenstein? Is that his real name or some kind of joke?"

Mara gives a half-grimace, half-smile. "Both, I fear," she says, with an apologetic shrug. "It was the name given to him by his creator who, from what I can gather, was rather..." She pauses, as if deciding how to properly word it, and then says, succinctly, "A piece of shit."

"Noted. And is he... How is his mental capacity?"

"He is sentient and mentally competent. As capable of thought and emotion as you and I." She pauses. "He was... unwell...when we first discovered the extent of his neglect and trauma, but I hope that is something that can be repaired with time."

I chew my lip, trying to consider what else to ask, but only one thing stands out. "Can I get a closer look?" I ask. And then, belatedly, "Is that safe?"

"I believe Dr. Wright intended for you to do an initial meeting and evaluation, if you're comfortable with that," Mara says. "We'll have him restrained for safety purposes."

A shiver of anticipation and nerves runs through me; I clasp my hands behind my back to stifle it. "I'm ready to get started as soon as he's prepped."

"Great," Mara says. "There's just one thing you should know before you go in, I think. X-14 is..." She pauses, seeming to consider how to word it. "He's technically...dead."

"...Dead?"

"Well, undead, I think is the correct term?" Mara shrugs. "But yes. He has no pulse."

I swear my own heart stutters. "That's impossible."

Mara only smiles. "See for yourself."

* * *

I snap on my rubber gloves and secure my medical mask with trembling hands.

I keep trying to tell myself to approach this as I would any patient, but I cannot stop replaying Mara's claim in my head, and with each repetition, the heartbeat in my ears grows louder. When it's clear I won't get any calmer than I am right now, I take a deep breath and turn to face the subject strapped to the medical table.

His arms are restrained tightly against his sides. A metal mask—I hate to think of it as a muzzle—covers the lower half of his face. His mismatched eyes track me, though the rest of his body is perfectly still, and he remains silent.

The MRF staff moved him into the "operation room," as they call it, for my initial evaluation. Something about the room is deeply off-putting. It's very clinical, with that type of powerful antiseptic smell that makes you wonder what exactly they're trying to cover up. White walls and white tile, cabinets, and a desk like a doctor's office. I'm used to the cold, impersonal nature of hospitals, but this atmosphere has a different, dangerous edge to it.

Perhaps it's the bed. The metal bed that X-14 is currently restrained to. Something about it reminds me less of a hospital room and more of a torture chamber. And X-14 is tensed, like he's bracing himself for the same.

A security guard stands on the other side of the table, his eyes never leaving the subject. Mara is here, too, standing against the wall behind me and observing. All of these safety measures...but it isn't just the potential risk that has my heart racing.

"Hello, Subject X-14," I say, stepping up to his side. I'm surprised to find that he doesn't smell like a corpse. He doesn't smell like a person either. There's a faint whiff of formaldehyde, likely only detectable because I'm so familiar with it. But stronger than that is a scent more like leather and the pages of old books. "My name is Lucy Sullivan. I'm here to assess your physical state. If you experience any discomfort at any time, please let me know." The words come out automatic, mechanical. I've never been very good with my bedside manner.

No response. He continues to stare at me. I clear my throat and take some of the tools waiting on the metal tray beside the table. No matter what Mara has told me about him, I'll feel better if I check everything myself, especially when he's such an unusual case. I need to make sure this isn't some sort of terrible misunderstanding or poorly conceived prank.

My heart thumps in my ears as I approach the table, every instinct screaming at me that I don't want to get too close to this...man, or monster; I haven't decided yet. But he stays still in his restraints, only his eyes moving to flick to the tools in my hands, taking them in one by one. Some of the tension in his shoulders eases, and I wonder what he was expecting to find me holding.

I take a deep breath and force myself to stand beside the table. "I'm going to begin by testing your vitals."

As I do, each test tells me the same thing that Mara did: this man is dead. Or should be, at least. He has no pulse, neither that I can find with my stethoscope on his chest nor with my fingers at his neck. His skin is cool to the touch, with that strange, almost silicone quality of the long dead—closer to the cadavers I've worked with than a living human. The sphygmomanometer gives no reading of blood pressure. He is not breathing. But his pupils react normally to light, and his mismatched eyes track me with clear alertness as I move around the table.

He is impossible, and yet he is here. Alive, or something like it.

As I step back from the table, stethoscope gripped tightly in my trembling hand, a wave of vertigo washes over me. My ears buzz and my knees falter; I have to grab the counter to hold myself upright. This is no prank or misunderstanding. It can't even be explained away as a medical anomaly. It's too far removed from the realm of logic and science to be called anything less than supernatural.

This man is alive, but not. He's dead, but conscious. It makes me feel small and unmoored, but also...something else, something harder to parse.

Images flash through my mind. My mother's limp hand clutched in my child-sized fingers. A young girl motionless on a hospital bed. The memories of two medical monitors, both flatlining, now overlapping and bleeding together in my memory.

A monitor of X-14's vitals would read the same, and yet. *And yet.* He's beaten it. He's beaten death.

I have to know how. *I have to understand.*

"Are you all right?"

Mara's voice drags me back to the present. I'm still gripping the counter with one white-knuckled hand, the other strangling the stethoscope. I force both sets of fingers to unclench and smooth my expression over before I turn to face her.

"Yes," I say. "Just...processing."

"I know it's a lot to take in." Her eyes are sympathetic. I almost want to take her up on the unspoken invitation to talk about it, but instead I turn back to my clipboard and dutifully record the impossible facts of X-14's vitals until my hands stop shaking.

I turn again to look at X-14, who stares at the ceiling. It's impossible to say how much cognition is going on behind those mismatched eyes. I'm desperate to find out more. But before I delve into him, I think of all of those doors I passed when we entered the facility. *X-11, X-12, X-13...*

"The subjects here," I say, looking at Mara. "Are they all like him?"

She shakes her head. "X-14 is unique. They all are. Each one is different." She pauses. "But each impossible in their own way, if that's what you're asking. They could each be considered"—a breath—"monsters, for lack of a better word."

"I see." More questions are on my tongue, but even thinking about new impossibilities gives me that sense of reality unraveling again. I swallow it and focus on the impossibility in front of me. "And how am I meant to help him?"

It feels strange to talk about him as if he isn't here, but X-14 is still stoic and silent despite Mara's claim that he's sentient.

"The main issue is that he's falling apart." She gestures to the lines of stitching, the bandaged stump of his left arm where his hand is missing. "He's not decaying like a corpse would— even the detached hand is still perfectly preserved—but his stitches are giving out. We'd like to address that so he can live more comfortably. Past surgeries indicate that if the hand is reattached, he'll regain full use of it almost immediately."

"I see." I glance at the spot where his hand should be, and back at Mara. "Can he speak?"

"When he wants to, yes. But I believe he's doing his best to ignore us, isn't that right, X-14?"

I swear I detect the faintest clench of a muscle in his jaw, but he makes no other response. Even that tiny movement is enough to make me shift away in warning. I don't understand how Mara can treat him so casually. Judging by the security guard's stance, he's more on the same page that I am.

The thought of approaching him again now that I *know* he's a walking corpse makes that sensation of unraveling swell again in my mind. Yet I take a deep breath and force it down. If I want to understand this—this *monster*—then I will need to overcome it. I force myself to take a step forward, and then another.

I lean in to get a closer look at the arm nearest to me, which is the left one, with the missing hand. I'll have to get under his clothing at some point for a full assessment, but hopefully he'll warm up to me before we get to that stage.

"How long ago did you lose your hand?" I ask. He doesn't answer. Part of me is itching to unwrap the bandages and take a better look for myself, but that seems like it would be beyond the bounds of this initial assessment. "And let's take a look at the leg you're having trouble with..." I wait for him to protest, or to speak at all, but there's still nothing. I carefully roll up one pant leg and suck in a sharp intake of breath as I see the state of his limb. A crude line of staples stretches across his calf, and they're barely hanging on. The lower part of his leg, ankle, and foot are twisted at an odd angle. Several of the staples have popped free already, and the rest will surely go soon. I'm surprised he can stand, let alone walk.

I don't know how his body operates—this is far beyond the rules of anatomy and logic that I know—but I can't imagine the missing and barely attached parts are good for his health. "Reattaching these parts may help you be more comfortable," I say, tracing my finger through the air above the jagged line of staples. "All of these repaired areas could be more secure, too. They seem..." I hesitate, trying to think of a nice way to say that these staples clearly weren't done by a medical professional of any repute. They seem amateurish and hasty. Almost as if... I blink, looking up to meet his eyes as a thought occurs to me. "Did you do these yourself?"

Unexpected movement catches my eye—his chest rising as he takes in air for the first time since I've started watching him.

"That obvious?" Even though it's distorted and tinny from the mask over his face, the gravelly sound of his voice sends a shiver through me. His voice is deep and rough. I can almost *feel* it reverberating through me.

It takes me a moment to realize I've taken a step back in my shock. I take a deep breath, clasp my hands behind my back, and shove my swirling thoughts and emotions down.

"To a trained eye? Yes. Though it's impressive you managed it at all," I tell him. He blinks up at me before looking away. But I forge ahead. "I'd like to take a closer look, see if there's any damage to the musculature. And of course I'll have to remove these staples before reattaching it..." I'm getting ahead of myself. I haven't taken the job yet, not officially. Still, I can't resist the urge to get a closer look. "Will it hurt if I touch the area?"

"It's fine." He breathes again. So he doesn't need oxygen to function, but he does need to fill his lungs with air to speak. *Fascinating.* All of it is as fascinating as it is horrifying, but I try to push aside that mental note and focus on his words, which introduce an entirely new concern to my treatment plan.

"That's not what I asked." He doesn't say anything more, so I venture, "If it hurts, I can give you something for the pain." I'm not sure if he can metabolize painkillers orally, or if an injection will work when there doesn't seem to be any blood flow, but maybe a topical spray will have some effect. "Do you know what painkillers are effective for you?"

He glances over at me again. "No."

"No, as in they don't work?"

"As in, I don't know."

My frown deepens. "Has no one ever tried to give you painkillers?"

He makes an awkward motion, probably a shrug, harbored by the restraints. His expression remains impassive. "Like I said, I can handle it."

I resist the urge to glance at Mara. She mentioned neglect and medical trauma, but that's now beginning to seem like a grave understatement.

"Well, that's unacceptable to me," I say. "My first order of business as your doctor will be finding a pain-reduction technique that's effective for you." I drum my fingers on the edge of the metal table, already thinking of the possibilities. I may not have officially accepted the job, but I'm itching to get started, to perform tests, to figure out how in God's name the impossibility in front of me operates.

No matter how badly I want to jump in feetfirst, that's not what I'm here for today. Yet Mara hasn't tried to pull me out yet, and I won't waste this chance to learn what I can. "I suppose for today I could get a basic understanding of your nervous system." Or whatever approximation of one he has. Do his nerves still fire when he's technically dead? I have no idea. So logic says I should start from the basics and work my way up. Before I can determine how to make him *stop* feeling, I should try to get a grasp of how—and to what extent—he feels at all. "Shut your eyes."

He stares at me for a moment. His gaze flicks to the security guard, to Mara, and back to me. When I just continue waiting patiently, he lets his eyes slide shut.

"I want you to tell me what you feel, and where, okay?"

He lets out a grunt of acknowledgement.

It's easier to make myself approach this time, though my skin still prickles with alarm when I'm near him. I take a scalpel from the tray and lightly press the flat of the blade against his collarbone. He flinches but then relaxes.

"Pressure," he mutters. "Near my shoulder."

"Good." I try it again against his cheekbone and receive a similar answer. It doesn't seem to matter much if I press light or hard against his skin; he responds to the feeling in much the same way. It's similar when I try pinching the skin of his arm between two of my gloved fingers. He doesn't seem to register the sensation much at all, other than "slight pressure."

There's no extra sensitivity near the lines of stitches. Nor is there any blood or discoloration. But the results of my tests do differ when I try the partially detached arm and leg. He doesn't seem to register sensation there at all, like they've been snipped off from whatever supernatural nervous system his undead body contains.

It's fascinating to try to figure out how his body works. I find myself wishing I had more tools. Different temperatures, different textures to test on him. Can he feel if something is hot or cold? There's only one way to test that at the moment, and my curiosity gets the better of me. After a moment's hesitation, I set down the scalpel, slide off one of my gloves, and press a finger against the side of his neck, near one line of stitches.

I watch the way his Adam's apple bobs, next to where I'm touching him. "Warm," he says. "On my neck."

And he feels cold beneath my touch. My heart is pounding at being so close to him, but I force myself to trail my finger down along the line of stitching, where it cuts between his collarbone.

I pause at where it disappears beneath his shirt, wondering how far it goes.

When my eyes lift to his again, I notice that he's opened them. He's watching me with an unreadable expression. I quickly recoil, step back, and place my glove back on. I flush as I remember that Mara and the security guard are still in the room, watching this interaction. I hope they didn't feel that same strange charge in the air as our eyes locked for a moment.

"This is a good start," I say, clearing my throat. "Next time I'll come prepared with better tools to assess your levels of sensation, but for now, I think we can call it a day." I meet his eyes and fight a shiver that slips up my spine. "It's nice to meet you, X-14."

He meets my gaze with his one blue eye and one brown but says nothing.

As I turn and walk out the door with my heart pounding, I realize two things. One, I'm going to have to shift my worldview to accept the fact of his existence. And two, I've never wanted anything as badly as I want the chance to figure out what makes this impossibility function.

Chapter Four

A stranger waits outside the lab. She's middle-aged, dressed impeccably in tailored trousers and a silk blouse, and more than a little intimidating.

"Ms. Sullivan," she says, nodding. "I'm Dr. Wright. Follow me."

I trail after the tap of her heels to her office and sink into the chair she offers while she sits behind the desk.

"So." She gazes at me, hands folded on her lap and posture ramrod straight. "You seem to be holding up well."

I'm not sure if I'd agree. My palms are slick with sweat as I press them against my skirt, and I feel lightheaded. Still, I force myself to nod.

"I'm sure you can understand now why we don't hire in the standard way," she continues. "Someone could have a beautiful résumé, conduct a perfect interview, and completely fall apart when faced with one of our subjects. There's nothing to be done but fly them in and see if they can handle it."

I flex my fingers in my lap and take a deep breath. "I can handle it." Despite my unease, the fraying of my understanding of the universe, I need it to be true. Because I will do anything it takes to get back into that room and have access to X-14.

Dr. Wright gives me a thin but encouraging smile. "I believe we will have a multitude of uses for an employee with your experience, but if you accept the offer, your main task will be ministering to X-14 and his physical difficulties. He's fallen into neglect, and his previous doctor was let go during our restructuring. After meeting your subject, how would you approach treatment?"

I cross my legs and consider the question for a few seconds. "I didn't have time to complete a full physical assessment. But the most obvious first order of business would be to repair his leg before he loses it. And then...do you still have the hand he lost?" She nods. "Then I would attempt to reattach it, since the stitches on his body suggest past operations have returned sensation and functionality to lost parts."

"And how would you approach such a surgery?"

"Well..." I think again, taking my time. Dr. Wright doesn't try to rush me. "Step one would be figuring out how to manage his pain." I fold my arms over my chest, wrestling with a surge of anger as I recount what X-14 told me earlier. Maybe I was wrong before. Maybe I wouldn't do *anything* to get this job, because I certainly won't do whatever has been done to him. "I'm not sure how this facility has been handling his procedures in the past, but I find it unacceptable that there was no attempt to use painkillers on him." Normally, I wouldn't insult my predecessor at a job, but I feel strongly enough about this that I don't care. If this is a deal-breaker for them, so be it; I will not compromise my morals for a job, even one I want as badly as this.

"Good." Dr. Wright pulls a piece of paper out of her desk. She signs it with a flourish.

I blink. "Yes, and then—"

"That's all I need to know," Dr. Wright says. "In the past, this facility has been focused on the imprisonment of, and experimentation on, the various subjects within. Now that I'm at the helm, I intend to move forward with the goal of rehabilitating our subjects and beginning to make up for the damage we have done. You've already said enough that I trust you would be a worthy member of our new team." She pushes the paper across the desk to me—it's a contract. "I believe that you'll do an exemplary job, Ms. Sullivan. We'd be pleased to have you on board, if you accept our offer." She sets her pen down and leans back in her chair.

I wish I could say that I hesitate. That I consider all of the red flags I noticed before I even met the patient I'm supposed to be working with. And yet, when faced with the impossible, how could I do anything other than try to understand it? I think of the wonder I felt when I pressed my fingers to his cold and pulseless neck, and I sign the contract without a second thought.

* * *

Everything moves quickly after that. The MRF helps me find an apartment and pays for the cost of my move. The next couple of weeks are a blur of packing and phone calls. And every time I lovingly wrap another one of my taxidermy creations in an ungodly amount of bubble wrap for the drive over to Arizona, I'm thinking of X-14. The impossibility and enigma of him, his scars and his stitches.

As I often do when I'm getting too invested in something, I get the thoughts out of my head by putting them down on

29

paper. *Research*, I call it, when I buy a notebook for the explicit purpose of writing things I know and want to know about him. Right now, most of what I write are questions; I take my pen and jot down new ones every time one pops into my head.

What does he eat, and how often? How does his system process food? How does his nervous system work? Does he feel some sensations more strongly than others? Are his eyes from different bodies—and if so, does the eyesight differ?

And of course, there is one bigger, more significant question: *how, and why, was he created in the first place?*

* * *

By the time I'm setting up my new apartment, I'm already a little in love with Ash Valley. I've been warned about the intensity of the summer heat in Arizona, but right now it's fall, and the weather is cool and dry and lovely. The desert is quiet, and without the light pollution of a city, the stars seem brighter and more plentiful than ever before.

I leave the window open while I carefully unwrap and arrange my taxidermy creations and install them around the room. This one-bedroom apartment is considerably larger—*and cheaper*—than my cramped studio in LA was, and I'm pleased to see how much space I still have left to fill.

In LA, I often felt like I was squeezed in so tightly, I couldn't breathe, surrounded by tall buildings and too many people. Here, I feel like I have room to relax. Room to grow.

I spend my night sitting by the open window, sipping a glass of wine and listening to classical music play as I gaze out at the silhouette of the facility on the horizon. Tomorrow I will enter those walls and face an impossibility once again, and I'm not sure if the sensation swirling in my stomach is excitement or fear.

31

Chapter Five

The next morning, I arrive at work ten minutes early with my notebook about X-14 in hand. Dr. Wright meets me—promptly this time—in the lobby.

"Welcome back, Ms. Sullivan," Dr. Wright says. "We're pleased to have you as a part of the team." With that, she sets off at a brisk pace to give me a tour of the building. She shows me the location of the break room, the bathrooms, and her office. I commit it all to memory even as my eyes wander to the innumerable doors we pass, searching for the X-14 that will designate my patient. We pass 11, 12, 13...and finally stop.

"This is Observation Room 14, which will serve as your personal working space," Dr. Wright says, opening it for me to show me the minimalistic interior. Just a metal desk, a single chair, and the viewing panel I initially glimpsed him through, though it's currently covered by metal shutters. "Room 14B, through that window, consists of X-14's...personal quarters." Since Mara already showed me, I can guess what the pause in her voice suggests; the room is little more than a cell. "You can observe and speak to him through here, though I expect much of your work will be done in the operation room. When you wish to take him there, speak to a security guard to have him prepped for transport."

I nod. We passed a few of the uniformed guards along the way, though not as many as I'd expect from a place like this. "Do I have access to 14B as well?"

"No," Dr. Wright says. "Until we complete our assessment of X-14's threat level, you can only be in the room with him after security has properly restrained and masked him. Only they have access to the room."

"But if there's some kind of medical emergency..."

"Then our security team will grant the most expedient—and safe—access possible. But your safety is our priority." Dr. Wright meets my gaze and smiles thinly. "I wouldn't worry. I assure you that there is little that could threaten X-14."

Part of me wants to ask how she knows that...but it feels almost accusatory to voice the question. Instead, I glance in at the room again, and my eyes are drawn to a folder sitting on the desk.

"Ah, yes," Dr. Wright says, following my gaze. "That would be X-14's file. You don't have clearance for all of the information, but I gave you as much as possible. We know little about his past before he entered the facility, I'm afraid, but have detailed notes about the years since he arrived. Including the incidents that have given us reason to approach him with caution."

"Mara mentioned a history of violence."

Dr. Wright nods. "Our previous policy would involve withholding details of his past from you, but I found that irresponsible. However, I will warn you the details in that folder are graphic."

My stomach flutters, equal part nerves and sick curiosity. But I push it away. "I would prefer to conduct my initial assessments without coloring them by anyone else's opinions, if that's all right."

Her eyebrows lift, but her expression is otherwise unchanged. "As you see fit. Is there anything else you'd like to know?"

I consider for a moment and shake my head. "I'm ready to work."

Her mouth curves in amusement. "Most people have plenty of questions."

I shrug, folding my hands behind my back. "I prefer to find my own answers." My gaze wanders to the observation room and that shuttered viewing panel. "And I suspect I'll find most of them by interacting with my patient."

Of course I'm curious about what else the building holds, as well—but for now, I find it prudent to focus on one mystery at a time. And a living corpse seems like more than enough of a mystery for me. I'm eager to be face-to-face with him again and learn more.

"I admire that, Ms. Sullivan, but know that my office door is always open to you." Dr. Wright's look is sharp, assessing. "Let me introduce you to one of our security guards, who can show you the precautions we're taking with X-14 and get him set up for today's session."

* * *

The security guard is a man in his thirties named Hunter Barnes. He's handsome, with dark eyes and dark stubble on a sharp jawline, and the distinctive slice of a scar across one cheekbone. He greets me with a firm handshake and an easy smile.

"I've been working with X-14 for the last couple of months," he says. "He hasn't given me any trouble, but we have to take precautions due to his history."

I nod. "Surely with the restraints and mask, I can have some privacy with him during our sessions?"

He considers. "I suppose I could wait outside of the room, if that's what you think is best."

"I do. I believe it's important for building a trusting relationship, and I need that to work effectively with him."

"I'm fine with that as long as he maintains his good behavior," Hunter says. "I'll get him set up now. You can either wait in the operation room or watch from the observation window."

I take him up on his offer to watch. It feels strange, peering in unobserved from behind the one-way mirror, but I want to get a better idea of both X-14's behavior and his interactions with this security guard. Hunter seems nice enough at first glance, but I can't shake my wariness of everyone in this building, especially given what I know about X-14's past treatment. It's impossible to forget that his former doctor conducted surgery on him without any attempt at painkillers, and that was allowed for God knows how long. I know Dr. Wright claimed things have changed, but like I told her, I prefer to form my own opinions based on what I observe.

The process of preparing X-14 is calmer than I would've expected. He stands against the wall while Hunter rolls a metal hospital bed inside. Hunter steps outside of the door again while X-14 puts on the metal face mask before climbing onto the bed. He attaches his own ankle straps, then lies back. Hunter enters again, restrains X-14's arms to his sides, and checks both the mask and the ankle straps.

No words are spoken aside from Hunter's brief instructions, and it all seems rather rote for both of them. X-14 is silent, his movements unhurried. It's a relief for me to see that after being warned about my patient's violent past, and makes me feel more certain about my preference for being alone in the room with him. But it's hard not to also notice just how thorough these precautions are. Every moment Hunter is in the room with X-14, his posture is stiff and his eyes alert, even when he's giving that disarming smile.

I wait for Hunter to transport the strapped-in X-14 to the operation room before heading there myself. I thank the security guard before walking into the room alone.

Chapter Six

My heart is pounding for a multitude of reasons as I pull on my gloves and safety goggles. I'm intensely aware that I am alone with X-14 for the first time. Alone with a walking corpse, an impossibility, a subject with a history of violence. *My patient.* I take a breath of antiseptic-scented air and school my expression into calm professionalism before I turn to face him.

"Hello again."

X-14 lets his head fall to the side so he can regard me through half-lidded eyes, his expression indifferent.

"You're back."

"Did you think I wouldn't be?"

He shrugs. His affect is all casual indifference, but he tenses up as I approach the table. His eyes flick to my hands, and then my face, before he relaxes a fraction.

Medical trauma, I remind myself. I keep my gloved hands in his sight so he knows I'm not carrying anything. "I'm going to start with a quick examination," I tell him.

Despite my nerves, there's only the slightest tremble in my hands; my adrenaline isn't going haywire quite as badly as it was the first time I met him. I suppose there's been enough time for the impossibility of his existence to sink in, so now I can make a more clear-headed approach.

His leg has grown worse, more of the staples having popped off so the lower leg is barely hanging on. And of course his hand is still detached, though there are no signs of further damage or decay as far as I can detect.

"You gonna put me back together?" he asks as I step back. Already chattier than last time. Perhaps because he's accepted that I'll be a more permanent facet of his care, or perhaps because he's beginning to trust that I'm here to help him. Hopefully both.

"Not quite yet," I say.

His brow furrows, a silent question.

"I won't operate until I can find a way to not hurt you while I'm doing it."

"I told you, it's fine."

"And I told you it's not. I'm not comfortable performing a procedure of that nature without any kind of anesthetic."

"And what if it's the only choice?" He sounds annoyed. "If you're not *comfortable*, just give me the tools and I'll do it myself."

"We're going to find a way," I say with more confidence than I feel.

He rolls his eyes, saying nothing.

I take a deep breath to steady myself. "Regardless. I'd like to gain a better understanding of your physicality before I perform any kind of operation. I'd like to do a full physical exam today, if that's all right with you."

He looks at me and blinks when he seems to realize I'm expecting a response. "Yeah, sure. Whatever."

"May I remove your clothes?"

I can't tell if he's smirking or if it's the jagged rip in his cheek that makes it look that way. He's silent until he realizes I'm waiting for an answer and sighs as if *I'm* the one being a pain in the ass. "Go ahead."

My heart is thumping as I carefully undo the buttons of his shirt, finally able to view the stitches that disappear under his clothes.

I've seen a lot of naked bodies before. I know how to approach these situations with professional detachment. But I must admit that out of all I've seen, nobody's body has been as intriguing as this one. His musculature is that of a lean, fit twenty-something, but his skin is the same patchwork of stitches and green skin as the rest of him. And with his full body exposed, it's clearer than ever that not all of these parts are from the same corpse. There are areas where the stiches hold together pieces that are not an exact fit.

I think, for a disconcerting moment, of approaching him like a taxidermy project. Choosing the best pieces to stitch together to create something entirely new...

That gives me a strange, queasy sensation, so I try to focus on his tattoos instead. There are plenty more to be seen on his body, a medley of skulls and snakes and geometric shapes. Plus a barbell pierced through his left nipple. Old scars and sutures mark his torso, including a puckered scar that runs from his sternum to his belly button, slicing through his visible abdominal muscles. I wonder who cut him open, when, and why. Was it before or after his reanimation? There is also a part of me that is itching to reopen him, to study his internal organs and how they're operating—but no, no, that's not why I'm here. There's no sign of deterioration or damage on his torso like with his leg and hand, so I move on.

"I'm going to undress you from the waist down now," I say. "I'll leave your undergarments."

"Mm–hm," he says, staring at the ceiling. At least he seems to have gotten the idea that I require verbal consent with each step.

I carefully peel off the baggy orange pants. He wears tight gray briefs beneath them. Try as I might, it is impossible not to notice a significant bulge beneath them, including a distinctive shape that I suspect may be a piercing of some kind. He appears to be partially erect—not that I'm looking.

"It's always like that," he says, as if following my train of thought. "Don't be too flattered."

"Hm, that's interesting," I say as neutrally as I can manage. No blood flow, but he can still get an erection. Perhaps some kind of rigor mortis? I make a mental note of it and move on to examine his leg. The more I look at it, the less I understand how it's operational when only a handful of strained staples are keeping the muscles of his thigh attached to the rest of the limb. Legs are a complicated weave of muscle; it doesn't make any sense that it can still function like this. But nothing else about him follows my understanding of anatomy either.

I press my gloved fingers to his calf. Goose bumps ripple down my arms at the sensation of his flesh, cool and strange. "Flex this for me, please?" He does, and rotates his ankle, and moves his toes, and a variety of other things to prove he can, indeed, still operate the leg perfectly fine.

When I pull away, I find him watching me with a curious look in his eyes.

"What?"

"Most people hate touching me." He tilts his head. That torn flesh in his cheek makes him impossible to read. Is it a smirk or a snarl in his expression? "But you don't."

I flush and straighten, pushing my glasses up my nose. "I apologize if I'm making you uncomfortable," I say. "I know you're not just some scientific experiment for me to play around with. I'm just so curious about how your body works."

The permanently curled side of his mouth drifts further upward in what is now *definitely* a smirk. "By all means, have your fill of me."

The heat in my face intensifies. I clear my throat and step back even further away from the table. Retreating, though I hate to think of it like that. "That's enough for an initial assessment."

Refusing to look at his expression to see if he's still smirking, I grab my notebook from the counter and flip to a new page so I can record my observations. I feel his eyes on me as I scribble down notes about his physical state, as well as several new questions to add to the list about how his body functions without blood flow. Finally, I snap my notebook shut and look up at him. "Now I'm going to test some sensory inputs and how your body responds to them. I'd like to gain a better understanding of how your nervous system operates before doing anything that may cause you pain."

"I can handle a little pain." He says it without bravado, like it's a clear fact, nothing more and nothing less. His expression is steady, stoic.

I study him. Surely this must be bluffing. "I assume that *stapling your hand back onto your body* would cause more than 'a little' pain."

"Nothing I haven't been through before, Doc."

I pause, leaning against the counter instead of returning to my work. Normally, I try to avoid probing personal questions—

no matter my curiosity, it's not part of my job description—but it's hard to resist the bait he's dangling in front of me. I recall our first meeting, and how I noted that many of his stitches seemed to be self-performed surgeries. "Did you not have a doctor to help put you back together in the past?"

He pauses for so long that I'm not sure he's going to answer. "My creator did, at one point." Anger darkens his expression, twisting his usually emotionless face until I hardly recognize him. "Till I stopped being her good little creation and she decided she was more interested in taking me apart. Then it was mostly up to me to pick up the pieces when she got bored."

I swallow back nausea. "That was before you ended up in the MRF, or...?"

He shoots me an incredulous look and huffs a laugh. "They don't tell you shit, do they?" he mutters. "No. The worst of it happened here. Before I came here, it wasn't...wasn't *so* bad. Till I started resisting her commands, and she realized I wasn't the meat puppet she wanted me to be. Then she decided she'd rather learn from taking me apart and putting me back together again." His jaw works, clenching and unclenching. "So she brought me here. Made some kind of deal with them. And of course the MRF was only too happy to let her do whatever she wanted if it meant they got their hands on me too."

I click my pen and let out a slow breath. "Well, she's gone now," I murmur. "And you have me. Things are going to be different."

* * *

When lunchtime arrives, I eat alone in the observation chamber next to X-14's cell. I barely taste the sandwich I packed, more focused on jotting down notes. Treating X-14 is a daunting task, especially given how little he seems inclined to help me figure this out. I can't trust that he'll be truthful when relaying his pain levels; he seems impatient to get this over and done with. But I refuse to rush. I'm not going to accept so easily that it's impossible to make this process comfortable for him. Especially because it sounds like no one has even *tried* before.

But as with any medical mystery, I'll just have to approach it logically. Even though his condition defies traditional logic, there has to be *some* rhyme or reason to the way his body works. Through trial and error, I'll figure out a way to treat him safely and comfortably for us both. I have to believe that, especially after what he told me about his creator and her treatment of him. This is the sort of job I was made to do, and X-14 is a patient in desperate need of a gentle hand.

As soon as I finish my meal, I cut my lunch break short and get back to work. That now consists of hunting down Dr. Wright to ask where I can find medical supplies.

Chapter Seven

When Dr. Wright opens the door to the medical storage room, all I can do is stare.

"Oh," I say.

"Yes, we're well-stocked," she says. It's an understatement. The walls are lined with shelves, each shelf stocked with anything I could think to ask for. It's like a full-on pharmacy in here, mostly consisting of heavy-duty anesthetics. As she continues to talk, I walk forward, reading labels, my mind already racing to consider which options to try first. "I'll ask security to add access to your ID card, but you can ask me for whatever you need until then. I trust your judgment. If there's anything we lack, let me know and I can order it in."

"Have any of these anesthetics been used on X-14 in the past?" I ask, still scanning labels.

"I believe some of them have been used to subdue him in the past," Dr. Wright continues. "Though not with success. Have you read his file yet?"

I pause, stiffening at the reminder of the *history of violence* Mara mentioned before. I had almost managed to forget. "No," I admit quietly. "I was under the impression some of the information may not be accurate or up-to-date anyway."

"That's likely true," Dr. Wright says. "Forming your own opinions is all well and good for your initial assessment, but I suggest reading through it at some point. It may help you better understand him."

"Noted," I say. I know that she's right, but for some reason I can't put my finger on, I'm not keen on the idea.

Dr. Wright must have left me at some point while I was staring at the shelves of supplies, because soon enough I look up and find that I'm alone. I spend the rest of my day scribbling potential tests in my notebook, and then all night eager to try my first experiment.

* * *

The next morning, I walk into the operation room with a small medical case. X-14 watches me from the table, masked and restrained as usual; his attention sharpens as he sees what I'm carrying.

"Good morning," I say.

He grunts.

I set the case on the counter, click it open, and show him the contents: a syringe and a small bottle of sedative. "With your permission, I'd like to begin trialing potential methods of analgesics for your surgery. This is propofol, a common general anesthetic. Enough of it to knock out a normal man of your size twice over."

The facility is well-stocked with injectable sedatives, so I decided that will be my first approach. I already suspect it won't work—how could anything move through his veins, with no heartbeat?—but it's worth ruling out. And it's always possible that I'll be surprised. He already defies biology in other ways, after all. There shouldn't be any way for his dick to get hard, either, but here I am with that knowledge seared into my brain for all of eternity.

But I'm not thinking about that.

"Don't bother. It isn't going to work," he says.

"You have experience with it?"

"If it's the same shit the security guards have tried injecting me with in the past, yeah. Doesn't work on me."

I bite my lip. Perhaps I should have read that file. "Well, I'd like to attempt my own test, all the same. It's possible it has some effect on you but you require a larger dose, or that your reaction could give some clue about what other methods may work." I pause, syringe in hand, and glance at him. "With your consent?"

He sighs. "Be my guest."

"Okay." I approach cautiously, keeping the tray close at hand. He's still given me no reason to fear him, and I know he's restrained, but being this close to him gives me an odd, shivery sensation. It's something about the coldness of his skin, the utter stillness of him, the way his eyes follow me without his head moving. It's not fear, exactly, but I am hyperaware of him every second.

I perform all the steps I would for any other patient: sanitizing his arm with an alcohol swab, prepping the needle, telling him to relax his muscles and take deep breaths as I search for a vein. Then I inject him with the sedative, my eyes flicking from the insertion site to his eyes watching me. His expression remains completely impassive as the needle sinks in, and his gaze doesn't flicker once. It should take effect immediately, but...

"Nothing," he says. There's no change in his voice or his expression. "Like I told you."

I sigh, remove the needle, and carefully wrap the area in gauze even though there's no blood welling up. "And like I told you, it's a necessary test." I realize, distantly, that my hands aren't shaky today. At some point, my body seems to have decided it isn't afraid of X–14 anymore.

With a normal patient, I'd be able to take his vitals to get a better sense of how his body is reacting, but of course, that's a moot point here. I do gauge his reaction time and check his pupils for dilation, but there doesn't seem to be any change.

I lower the flashlight from his eyes. "Okay. That's all for today. I can't risk muddling the results or the threat of a delayed reaction."

His brow furrows. "Seriously?"

"Of course. I'm going to be careful with your well-being, as I would with any other patient."

"But I'm not just any patient. I can take it. You're wasting time."

I bite back a retort, set aside the flashlight, and take a seat with my notebook in my lap.

There isn't much I can do as far as running tests today, but that doesn't mean I can't gain important information. "I'd like to circle back to something you mentioned. You said that security here had tried to knock you out with sedatives before?"

"Mm," he says, which I take as an affirmative.

"When was that? And why?" When he hesitates, I continue. "I've never seen any signs of violence from you, but given the precautions they insist on taking, I take it there's a reason?"

He shrugs, looks away. "You'll see it eventually, Doc. And then you'll know."

An eerie sense of foreboding prickles across my senses. "Know what?"

He stares at the ceiling with a flat expression. "What I really am."

Chapter Eight

Testing painkillers is a slow process, especially since I have no idea what will or won't affect X-14. I can't risk overdosing him or muddling my results by mixing medications, so I decide on a plan of action that involves trying one method per day. It's the safest way to go about things.

But it also leaves a frustrating amount of waiting in between tests.

Part of me wants to fill it with conversations with X-14, but I know it's not fair to keep him strapped to a chamber in the operation room all day just so I can satisfy my curiosity. Especially because he grows moodier as the days go on. He seems to revert back into his shell, growing snappish and impatient, and then barely responding like he did the first time I met him. I can only imagine it's because he's angry with me for not going ahead with the surgery like he wants me to.

So instead of holding him there in the operation room, I let him return to his own room as soon as I'm satisfied he isn't having any adverse reactions, and retreat to my observation room.

I rarely open the window to look into his adjacent space; it feels like an invasion of privacy. Instead, I sit in the small room, in a silence broken only by the occasional thump from X-15's room next door, and write in my notebook test results, or ideas for new trials. Sometimes I catch myself just doodling my patient; I cannot seem to let go of my fascination with his physical appearance. Occasionally, I force myself to steal glances at X-14's file. I still haven't managed to do more than flip through it. Something about it is very off-putting.

I'm trying again, my eyes hovering on the first page reading "X-14: The Revenant," when a knock at the door startles me. My first, immediate thought is that it must be Dr. Wright. Perhaps she's dissatisfied with progress so far, or lack thereof. I brace myself for an argument as I say, "Come in."

Instead of Dr. Wright's stern face, it's the younger woman I met when I first arrived. Mara Vance, unless I'm mistaken.

"Hi. Lucy, right?" She smiles at me while I nod, still wary. "Sorry to bother you, but I was wondering if you wanted to join me and some of the others for lunch in the break room. We're all curious about you. But no pressure, of course! Just figured I'd offer."

I almost reject her out of habit, but then I hesitate. As much as I enjoy my usual routine of eating in my office in silence and thinking about my work, I have to admit I'm curious about the other people who work here—and more so, about the subjects they work with. My focus is still on X-14, but I feel like I've accepted his existence enough that learning about other impossibilities won't break my brain.

"Sure," I say, gathering my things. "I have some time."

I only had a brief look at the break room when I first toured the facility. It's about what I'd expect a break room to be—three round tables, some uncomfortable-looking metal chairs, a tiny kitchenette. About half a dozen people are already in the room, security guards muttering over cups of strong-smelling coffee and what I suspect to be other scientists sitting quietly. Mara and I take the empty third table and are soon joined by a young blonde woman and Ezra, who gives me a cheerful nod. I have the impression this is an everyday thing for them and try not to feel like an outsider as I carefully unwrap my sandwich and salad.

Despite my misgivings, my curiosity gets the better of me. I manage to tolerate the introductions and small talk for about five minutes before I blurt out, "What kind of subjects are you working with?"

I'm not prepared for the awkward silence afterward. For a moment, everyone looks at me, and then at each other, and then Mara lets out a small laugh that breaks the tension.

"God, right, I'm still not used to that policy change," she says. "Not so long ago, we weren't allowed to talk about our subjects at all."

"Even to others working here?" I ask, puzzled.

"Yeah. They were pretty intense about the rules."

I frown. "Seems counterintuitive. I'm sure all of us have skills that could benefit a number of subjects, so the idea of restricting us to only one seems a bit ridiculous."

"Right?" Mara asks. "That's part of the reason I pushed for the change when Dr. Wright did the big overhaul." She clasps her hands on her lap. "So...right. I work with X-13. He's officially called 'The Nightmare,' but I generally just call him Somnus. He's a, um... well... a shadow creature who we think may have inspired stories of sleep paralysis demons. Mostly, these days I help welcome new hires, and Somnus and I both provide support in the facility where necessary."

I nod. I have about a million questions, both about the

nature of this so-called Somnus and what this 'support' entails, exactly. But after my question, I'm not sure where it's safe to tread in this conversation, so I stay quiet.

"I work with X-12," the quiet young woman named Belle speaks up when we look at her. "The Siren." She doesn't offer any more information than that, though the pink in her cheeks says there's more to be said.

"Is it going well?" Mara asks.

Belle hesitates. "We're making progress. Slowly. Earning her trust has been a process."

"I imagine so," Mara says. She glances at me. "A lot of the subjects here have suffered considerable trauma. This place used to be *rife* with assholes." She spears a bite of her food with perhaps more force than necessary. "Worse than assholes, honestly. It was rife with sociopaths."

Thinking back to what I know about my predecessor, I'm inclined to agree. "Dr. Wright mentioned there had been a significant overhaul of staff and procedures," I say.

"Yeah. She's been doing great work," Mara says. "But it'll be a process, earning back the subjects' trust. This place used to be one part prison and one part lab, and they were viewed as nothing but experiments."

"And what would you consider this place now?" I ask.

She twirls her fork in her hand, thinking about it. "Good question. Right now, I think, we're focused on understanding and rehabilitating our subjects. One day, I hope that we can even consider setting them free." Catching the look on my face, she quicks adds, "The subjects who are harmless, anyway. Because some of them are. Which is why it's so important to do our current assessments and make sure our files are accurate and up-to-date."

"I see." I think again of that file sitting on my desk, the sense of foreboding every time I open it. The history of violence that hangs like a black cloud over Victor, though I've never felt like he was a threat to me. Even if he *is* harmless, will he ever be ready to face the world? And will the world be ready for him? The thought sends a shiver down my spine, though it's hard to put my finger on why.

"Sorry, I'm getting way off topic," Mara says. "I'll shut up now. Ezra, tell us about your subject. Er, *subjects*, right?"

The sole man at the table is Ezra, whom I briefly met when he picked me up from my hotel. He smiles as our focus shifts to him. "Correct. I'm working with a variety of subjects classified as ghosts or spirits. But my primary focus right now is on X-15, who we're not really sure how to classify. He was initially indicated to be a poltergeist, but he has some distinct characteristics that make me wonder if he might be something else entirely, so I'm trying to get in contact with..." He pauses as he notices everyone gaping at him, and blinks. "What?"

"Sorry, did you just casually drop that *ghosts* are real?" Mara asks, mirroring my thoughts. "Jesus Christ, Ezra! You can't confirm the existence of life after death over a work lunch!"

Ezra rolls his eyes. "Come *on*, it can't really be *that* shocking when you've been working with a creature who *infiltrates your dreams*—"

"He what?" I ask, startled.

"Okay, but at least he's corporeal—"

"X-15 is remarkably solid most of the time, which is one of the reasons I think he's been misclassified—"

"Most of the time?" I repeat, thinking of the occasional heavy thumps I hear from X-15's cell next door, and the *emergency* on the first day I arrived here.

I can feel a headache coming on. I thought learning about my coworkers' subjects would help me gain a better understanding of what exactly happens in this place and what it means about my understanding of the world as I know it, but this is just making me more confused. I've been thinking of X-14 as a medical anomaly, mostly to salvage my own sanity, but with this new information, it might be time to accept that I'm dealing with something more akin to the paranormal.

Since X-14 has already proved the impossible, I can accept things like sirens—or werewolves, vampires, who knows—into my worldview, but *ghosts* and *nightmares* are something else entirely. It makes me feel like I'm teetering on the verge of some great fall. I've been struggling to wrap my mind around X-14's existence already. Fitting beings that aren't even corporeal into my worldview could make my perception of reality shatter entirely. Trying to understand this place and these monsters might just drive me insane...

While Ezra and Mara are still bickering about whether or not her own Nightmare can be classified as corporeal, Belle glances over at me and offers a small smile. "So what is your subject like?"

"Oh... X-14, the Revenant. Or Victor. I'm providing medical treatment, most importantly an upcoming surgery to reattach some parts that have been...well, detached." Her eyes widen, and I add, "He's mostly like you or me, but his body operates a bit differently. I'm still figuring out the finer details. But he's just an undead human, as far as I can tell."

Belle blinks at me. "Oh," she says. "Just that, huh?"

After a moment, a smile creeps across my face as the absurdity of the situation sinks in, and we both have to stifle our laughter.

Chapter Nine

Just when I'm starting to find a routine, one morning I approach the operation room and I know, instantly, that something is different.

A security guard is standing outside the door, and he immediately steps forward to intercept me before I can head in.

"Something's up with X-14."

I'm surprised by the immediate intense concern I feel. "What do you mean? Is it his leg?"

"No. But he doesn't seem like himself. I was about to go get Barnes."

I pause. Caution would dictate getting more information, waiting for Barnes, asking this security guard to come into the room with me. But I can't help but think of the facility's past, and how hard I've worked to build trust with Victor. I don't know this man, and I barely know Barnes. "He's restrained?"

The man nods reluctantly. "Yes, but—"

"Stand by. Let me take a look." I brush past him and walk in, unease churning in my stomach.

I pause as the door shuts behind me. X-14 is tense in his restraints. As I step closer, concerned that he's in pain, he jerks against the bindings and lets out a low sound in his throat, almost a growl.

"Stay back," he rasps.

I don't need to be told twice. His eyes are rolling, and there's an unfamiliar, almost animal look on his face. "What's wrong? Are you hurt?"

"No." His head jerks to the side so his face is angled away from me, his hands clenched and trembling. "It's—smell."

"What?"

He sucks in a breath and shudders it out. "Your. Smell." His body twitches, head jerking to one side and teeth braced in a grimace, and his arms writhe and strain against their restraints.

My brow furrows. I give myself a discreet sniff but can't detect anything unusual. It's interesting that he even has a sense of smell when he doesn't breathe, but I suppose he has to inhale to speak. Now that I'm looking more closely, I see the rapid rise and fall of his chest, a stark contrast to his usual stillness. He drags in breaths through his nose like he can't help himself. "I apologize if it's unpleasant."

"No." He lets out that low sound again, half *pain* and half *want.* "Smell...good."

The hair prickles on the back of my neck. Every instinct in my body screams at me to run, but I suppress it. I don't understand what's happening, but I do know that whatever it is, it's hurting X-14. Making him act half out of his mind. This is my patient and he needs me, so I force myself to take a step toward him. "What's going on? How can I help you?"

He snarls something wordless through his gritted teeth. His eyes roll back, and his fully attached arm strains so hard that the stitches begin to pop out of his skin.

"Victor!" I barely even register that I defaulted to his

name rather than the usual *X-14*. "Stop, you're going to hurt yourself!" I rush forward without thinking. Just as I reach the side of the table, his fingers twist and crack and *rip* free of the restraints, leaving his arm attached to his body with only a precarious handful of stitches.

At least two of his fingers are twisted, broken—but his hand is still strong enough to grab me by the throat.

My gasp cuts off as his grip restricts my airflow. I try to say his name, but no sound comes out. I claw desperately at the hand gripping me, but there's no reaction. When I roll my eyes to look down at him, I see nothing but animal hunger in his mismatched eyes.

He yanks me closer to where his head is still restrained flat against the table, and his teeth click inches from my face. A scream rises in my throat but dies where he's compressing my windpipe. The only thing saving me from his gnashing teeth is the metal mask still over his face. My cheek is pressed flat against the grate. He lets out a muffled snarl through it, a feral sound that has no business coming from a human.

It instills a terror deep in my core. The old, instinctual fear of prey facing a predator. In desperation, I scrabble a hand along his chest until I find the thick line of sutures that spans the length of his torso and dig my fingers into the old wound as hard as I can.

X-14 lets out a shocked little grunt. He abruptly shoves me away from him and releases his grip on me. I stumble and fall to the floor, sucking in air in deep, desperate gasps to fill my screaming lungs.

A moment later, the door bursts open and the security guard steps in. He pushes himself between me and X-14, one hand reaching for the baton at his waist.

"It's all right," I gasp out through my raw throat. "He's restrained—"

Even as I say it, I hear an awful sound, a tearing, cracking noise. I peek around the legs of the security guard to see X-14 thrashing on the table, his spine contorting at an impossible angle. His body twists toward us, his features contorted in a snarl beneath the mask and his eyes dead. He keeps twisting till his stitches pop and his left shoulder jolts free as half of his arm rips off. He sits upright on the bed, straining against the remaining restraints holding his wrist and ankles.

I scramble backward on the floor, one trembling hand fumbling for the door, though I can't keep my eyes off the monstrosity X-14 has become.

I'm not sure if it's bravery or something else that drives the security guard to step forward rather than back and pull his baton from his belt. He delivers a sharp crack of a blow to X-14's jaw.

X-14's head snaps to the side. And when he turns back, his jaw is hanging loose from his face, and so is the metal mask. He lunges toward the stunned security guard, who raises his arm to defend himself, and X-14's broken jaws latch on to his forearm.

The security guard screams. He wrenches himself backward and tears loose, leaving a chunk of flesh behind. I swear I can hear X-14 swallow from across the room.

Somehow, even while my ears ring and my head spins, I manage to scramble to my feet. I grab the shoulder of the shrieking, horrified security guard and pull him toward the door with me. Even as we rush out, I hear X-14 snarling and thrashing on the table like some mindless, rabid animal.

There's chaos in the hallway outside, a uniformed security

team rushing toward me with a white-faced Dr. Wright in their midst.

"Do not go in there!" I shout at them, before turning my attention to the security guard bleeding all over the white tile of the hallway. "Sit. Here." I help him to a seat and then yank my blazer off and press it to his arm. My stomach clenches at a glimpse of white bone through all of the gushing red, but I keep my head. "Apply pressure. I'll be right back."

I stand and nearly run into Dr. Wright in my haste to head to the medical supply room.

"Ms. Sullivan, are you all right?" she asks.

"I'm fine," I say, my voice coming out raspy from my bruised throat. Right now, I feel nothing but impatience at how it holds me back; I'm still pumped too full of adrenaline for the pain to set in. "This man needs medical attention—"

Dr. Wright turns and snaps her fingers at one of the security guards. "Emergency first aid kit. Now." He rushes off to obey her, and Dr. Wright grabs me by the arm as I try to follow. "No, you sit. Explain what happened."

"No, I'm fine, I—" My gaze snags on a man approaching the door to the operation room, and I snap, "Do *not* go in there."

He looks uncertainly at Dr. Wright, who nods. "It's on lockdown until we understand the situation. See to it." Then she looks back at me, and says, "Explain."

I do my best to, in stuttering sentences. I pause halfway through when someone rushes back with the first aid kit, but Dr. Wright's hand stays clamped on my shoulder and one of the other guards begins administering emergency aid to the wounded man. Once I realize he's adequately trained, I let my shaking legs lower me to the floor, and I stay there.

"I don't understand," Dr. Wright says. "He hasn't displayed

any violent behavior since the staff changeover. I assumed—perhaps erroneously—it was all a result of his mistreatment at their hands, but..."

"He didn't seem himself." My voice is barely a whisper, and even that hurts. "Like he wasn't in control of his body." I squeeze my eyes shut, trying to think back over what happened in that room, even though my brain tries to pull away from those memory. "He said... He said I smelled..." My eyes fly open and fix on Dr. Wright again. "He's hungry."

Her eyes widen, but then she shakes her head. "He's been fed regularly. I'm certain of it. There's no reason—"

"Well, whatever he's being fed didn't work," I snap, interrupting her. "He wouldn't have said anything because he... He never advocates for himself; he just accepts it. But we need to find him something else to eat."

She gives me a long look and nods. "Fine. I'll see what I can do. But you need to stay out of that room until I say otherwise."

I massage my neck and shoot a look at the security guards still clustered around the door to the operation room. "As long as they do too. Nobody approaches my patient without me."

Chapter Ten

Multiple people try to drag me off to receive medical treatment, but I insist on heading into the observation chamber next to the operation room instead. Dread is thick in my stomach as I sit at the desk and look through the one-way mirror at my patient.

X-14 is still on the table, the remaining straps on his ankles and right wrist keeping him secure. The other wrist restraint dangles loose with his detached arm hanging from it. His metal mask hangs off his face, half attached. He seems less agitated than he was before, but it still makes my gut clench when I see the drying rusty-red stains around his mouth.

I swallow. Perhaps I should leave it alone, but... I scan the desk until I find an intercom button and press it.

"Victor?" I say, my voice barely a whisper.

His head jerks up and toward the mirror. It's both painful and relieving to see *him* when I look at his face, lucidity back in his eyes. "Lucy." Not *Doc*, for once, and his voice is agonized. "I hurt you."

"I'm all right," I say.

"But I—"

"You're the patient here. Let's talk about you. I take it

whatever they've been feeding you has not been sufficient for your dietary needs."

He shuts his eyes and shakes his head. Less like an answer to my question and more like he's trying to warn off a nightmare.

"Focus," I say. I need him to stay with me, not lose himself to hunger again. "Tell me what you need."

"Meat," he groans, and a shudder runs through his body again, a violent tremor against the metal table. "F-flesh…"

I swallow hard, refusing to let myself feel afraid as I flash back to the sound of his teeth ripping into the security guard's arm. The sound of those teeth snapping just inches from my face, only the metal mask saving me from meeting a worse fate than that guard.

I focus on breathing, thinking. When I remember what he said about my smell, another ripple of horror flows through me, but I try to focus on the practicality of it. In order for him to eat, someone has to bring him food. But I can't vouch for the safety of whoever is in there. "It seems I can't safely approach you while you're like this. Is it just me whose—" I swallow again, convulsively, painfully. "Whose scent is bothering you?"

A jerky shake of his head. "Yours. Especially."

"Okay. Is there anyone who you think can safely approach you?"

He groans again, his body twisting and jerking, teeth grinding, half-attached arm dragging short nails against the metal table almost as if it has a mind of its own. "No. Not safe. I-I—" He stops, shakes his head as if trying to clear it. "Wait…Wait. There is one… I met her once…"

* * *

"What do you mean?'" Mara asks, affronted, when I break the news to her. I guess I could've explained it more gently, but I don't have the time for social niceties when X-14 is half out of his mind with hunger. What's important right now is getting him a meal, and quickly.

Mara sniffs herself without any self-consciousness. "I smell fine! Right? Tell me I smell fine."

I give her a small sniff at her insistence. "You smell fine to me. But X-14 insisted your scent is... 'nonhuman,' I think he said."

"That's even worse! What does that mean? What does a nonhuman smell like?!"

"Like smoke, he said."

Her eyes widen as if in realization, though it sounded like utter nonsense to me. I don't detect any whiff of smoke on her; she smells like sweet perfume, all flowers and vanilla. "Ahh," she says. "I think I know what he means."

"Feel free to elaborate at any time," I say, impatient. "I'd love to be able to approach him without him wanting to eat me."

"We might be able to arrange that." She gestures for me to follow and heads down the hallway.

I sigh and follow. "Are you going to tell me what this is about?"

She shoots an enigmatic smile over her shoulder. "I think it's time to introduce you to my partner," she says. "You can call him Somnus."

A chill trickles down my spine. I remember our lunch conversation. Somnus, the *Nightmare*, who infiltrates peoples' dreams. I'm not sure I'm ready to meet such a being, but I have to be, for Victor's sake.

Mara leads me into her office. It's small and messy. The desk holds scattered files and books, including a few about American Sign Language, which strikes me as odd. There are also several dirty coffee mugs and a vape. I lift an eyebrow at her, but she only shoots me a sheepish look and walks past the desk.

There's a door on the far side of the room, left slightly ajar. Something about it draws my eye. The darkness revealed through the opening is deep, untouched by the fluorescent lighting of this room. That darkness has an almost tangible quality. It's like a dream of darkness, a child's idea of darkness, solid and alive and ready to grab you if you venture too close. I can't seem to take my eyes off it.

Mara steps between me and the door, clasps her hands, and meets my eyes so I'm forced to look away from it. "Okay," she says. "Please keep an open mind."

"Just what I love to hear before meeting someone," I mutter, giving her a suspicious look.

"I promise he's not dangerous."

"Ah. Better and better."

"Yeah, okay, I'm making a mess of this. But please just...trust me? I think you've learned by now that not everything—and not *everyone*—in this place is as it appears to be." She holds out a hand.

I hesitate. This is all...very strange. But she's right—this place is full of strangeness. Including my patient, who needs me. If there's a chance this could help him, I have to take it. After a moment, I reach out, clasp Mara's fingers in mine, and let her lead me back into the darkness.

The only lighting comes from the thin sliver beneath the door as it shuts behind us. This room appears empty aside from us and some sparse furniture. A bed, a bookshelf, a table with two chairs. Like a cushy little apartment, tucked into the side of Mara's office.

"Somnus?" Mara's voice is quiet. "This is my friend Lucy. I'd like to introduce the two of you if that's okay."

The darkness moves. That's the only way my brain knows how to describe what happens. The shadows shift, even though nothing in the room is moving. I go still, a chill zipping up my spine in sudden, instinctive fear, like I'm in the presence of something dangerous. I catch myself holding my breath and have to force myself to stop.

The shadows draw up and form together into a humanoid shape a head taller than me, standing beside me and Mara. It turns to face me and I can't stop gawking. Then, absurdly, the shadow holds out a hand to shake.

Mara looks at me expectantly. I hesitate, gulp, and then reach out to grasp his shadowy hand. He's surprisingly tangible—and warm. Soft like velvet. There's a distant buzzing in my ears, and I hear Mara's brief conversation with him only as muffled, distant sounds.

"Close your eyes for a moment," Mara says, and I squeeze them shut obediently, hoping with a child's logic that when I open them again, everything will be normal. Something darts over my skin, quick and surprisingly warm, squeezing like a warm blanket for a moment before disappearing again.

"Okay," Mara says. "I think that should take care of your scent."

I slowly open my eyes and immediately search for the shadowy figure. He's still here, but standing back against the wall, like he knows I'm afraid of him. The thought makes me feel guilty.

"Thank you," I say, with only the slightest tremble in my

voice as I force myself to meet his eyes. He inclines his head in a slight nod.

Mara is smiling when I look at her again. "You did pretty well," she says, leading me out into her office again. "Most people scream when they see him for the first time."

I press a hand to my chest, feeling the way my heart is still racing. "I can't claim to have kept my cool, either."

"Still." She shrugs. "Thanks for keeping an open mind. He's really a big sweetheart."

Her voice is surprisingly tender. I think again of the way that room was connected to her office. Her connection with the shadow creature seems...a little more than professional. I am *so* tempted to pry, but right now there's a more pressing matter. "So you think I should be able to approach Victor now?"

"I think it's worth a try. Unless you want to send Somnus in instead—"

"No," I say firmly. "He's my patient. My responsibility."

"It's also the MRF's mistake that he wasn't fed properly," Mara says. "This is not within the range of responsibilities expected of you. You don't need to feel obligated, especially if you feel unsafe—"

"He's my patient," I repeat, more sharply than intended. I pause and take a breath. I know she means well, that she's just trying to help me, but she doesn't understand that this isn't about obligation. I need to get in that room again, to reassure myself and Victor that this can still work...and because of my worry that anyone else will only screw it up. "I appreciate your concern and your help," I tell her, "but this is my job. A job I want to do well. And Victor deserves a familiar face and a gentle hand right now. He's hurting."

Mara's wounded look softens. "You care about him."

"Of course I do," I say, willing my face not to heat up. "Like I said. He's my patient. I have to care to do my job well."

* * *

When I return to the hallway outside of the operation room, Dr. Wright is back as well, along with an older man I don't recognize. The moment I lay eyes on the man, I find that there's something unsettling about him, though I can't put my finger on what. He's a middle-aged man, well-groomed and objectively attractive, but his eyes are unsettling. When they shift to meet mine, I quickly look away, and down at the tray he's holding. It holds an array of raw meat, ranging from a cut of steak to ground beef to a slimy chicken breast to something gray and wet that I wish I didn't recognize as brain tissue. My stomach flips, and I swallow back nausea.

The moment she sees me, Dr. Wright shakes her head. "You're not qualified for this. Let us handle it."

I stand firm, my head tall. "Is anyone qualified? Does anyone in the building have experience hand-feeding X-14?"

Silence answers me. I take a step forward. "That's what I thought."

"Well, you're not going in alone," Dr. Wright says. She gestures to the man beside her, who is still watching silently with those strange, pale eyes. "Ms. Sullivan, this is Director Ramsey."

My confidence crumbles a bit. "Director...?" I blink, focusing on him. I've only heard the name but never met the man who's apparently in charge of this whole facility. It doesn't sit well with me that he came to handle this himself; I don't trust him.

"With all due respect, Director, your presence is just going to make things worse. The smell will drive him crazy. I've handled my scent"—*hopefully*—"so I'll be fine." *Theoretically...*

"That will not be a problem." The director's voice is very formal, and a bit odd.

Before I can ask what he means, Dr. Wright adds, "It's nonnegotiable."

I want to argue further, but I'm already aware of how much time I'm wasting standing here while Victor continues to starve his way to madness inside the room. "Fine. Just stay out of my way." I hold out my hands for the tray. After a moment and a glance at Dr. Wright, Ramsey hands it over.

There's a tense pause when I wonder if Dr. Wright is going to push harder against this. Yet after a moment, she waves a hand and a helmeted security guard moves to open the door. The guard enters first, hand on his gun, but nobody stops me from walking in behind him, with Ramsey trailing behind me.

X-14 is much like he was when I left him, half-restrained and bloody-mouthed. His head swivels to follow the security guard as he steps around the corner. He lets out a growl low in his throat, baring his teeth like a rabid dog. My stomach twists as I see him like this, but I clench the tray harder to stop my hands from shaking, and I gather my resolve.

"X-14." I wait for his eyes to snap to me and step closer so that the smoky heat of Somnus's scent will hopefully distract him from the human smells that stoke his appetite. "Here. For you." His eyes shift to follow me instead, though there's an eerie emptiness to them again, like he's not really seeing me. But they focus on me once I have his attention, and he doesn't seem to register Ramsey at all. His still-attached hand scrapes at the metal table at his side, fingers twitching in a motion that looks convulsive, uncontrollable.

I suppress a shiver as I set the tray on a nearby table and grab a pair of medical gloves. They're flimsy protection, but there's no time to waste in getting something better. "Victor," I say, hoping the tremor in my voice isn't too noticeable. "I'm going to remove your mask. I need you to try to restrain yourself. Do you understand me?"

No response. Nothing but the painful scrape of his nails on metal. I glance at the security guard standing tense at my side, and at Ramsey, who is watching this all with a curiously calm expression. Then I approach Victor and reach for the clasp of his mask. He's gone perfectly still, his hand no longer scraping, but it is not a comforting stillness, rather a watchful one that makes goose bumps ripple down both of my arms.

But at least he's not trying to bite me. Rather than reach over him and put myself too close to the vicinity of his teeth, I walk around the table and undo the other strap from that side, then quickly pull the mask off. My hands are shaking so bad that I drop it, and it clatters to the floor.

The silence afterward is loud. I can hear Victor's breathing, fast and hard, like the panting of someone who's run a mile. He doesn't usually breathe—and it's only when I see the flare of his nose that I realize he must be *smelling*.

I'm all too aware of the rapt attention of the security guard and Director Ramsey, both of them tense and ready to spring into action. I'm keenly aware of the gun at the guard's hip, the promise of violence if this doesn't go well. I need it to go well. This moment could either fix or permanently break the trust between me and Victor, and I *need* him to trust me if I'm going to have any hope of fixing his body. This will all fall apart without trust.

"Good, Victor." I reflexively fall into the soft, soothing tones of someone speaking to a cornered animal. I hate that I keep thinking of him like this, but there is nothing human in his expression right now; his face is a rictus mask, barely recognizable. It strikes a chord of fear within me even as I try to fight it. Still, I power through, crossing over to the tray, lifting the plastic spoon—*smart, no sharp objects*—and take a scoop of the raw ground meat. I walk over to him and will my hand not to tremble as I lower the spoon toward his mouth. "Okay," I say. "Let's take this slow—"

His head jerks up so fast, a stitch pops on his neck. His mouth closes over the meat, the spoon—reaches for the tips of my gloved fingers—

And all of a sudden I'm yanked backward so fast that my head spins. There's an arm around my waist. Director Ramsey, holding me off the ground one-armed with no effort whatsoever. Director Ramsey, who somehow moved across the room faster than Victor could bite down. I blink up at him, disoriented and dizzy and beginning to panic as I realize how close I just came to losing my fingers.

"I'm all right," I say, my voice coming out whispery through my tightened, still-raw throat. But I know that it's a lie. There are tears rushing to my eyes, and I can't seem to stop shaking.

I can't do this. I thought I could, but I can't, nor can I seem to bring myself to voice that.

"I will handle it." Ramsey sets me down, still coldly inexpressive, and turns his back to me as I sink back against the wall.

"Dr. Sullivan?"

I blink, trying to focus. My eyes can't seem to make sense of anything; the world is a blur of noise and confusion.

"Dr. Sullivan," a man's voice says again, and a warm hand grips my arm. I focus on the scar slicing across his cheek and recognize him. Hunter Barnes, the security guard. He must've removed his helmet to talk to me.

"Not a doctor," I manage to mumble out.

His lips quirk into a smile. "Ms. Sullivan. Breathe."

I do as he says, a quick in-out, and then a slower one, and the ringing in my ears fades.

"Good," he says. "Are you hurt?"

I shake my head and he squeezes my arm.

"Okay," he says. "Now, I'm going to need you to leave the room while we handle the situation here."

Despite the panic I'm barely holding at bay, a protest rises to my lips. "But my patient—"

"Is in good hands, I assure you, Ms. Sullivan." His voice is low and gravelly and serious. Something about it makes me want to trust him. He never takes his dark eyes off mine. "I assure you that I will personally look after X-14 for you."

"His name is Victor."

The man nods, his face softening. "I'll look after Victor. I promise. We'll get him fed."

I swallow hard and manage a nod. He offers me a big, calloused hand, and I take it and let him pull me to my feet and escort me to the door. I'm distantly aware of Victor still thrashing and snapping his teeth on the other side of the room, but I try my best to block it out. I try, too, to block out the trembling in my hands and the tightness in my throat.

Before I exit the room, I turn and clutch at the security guard who's been so kind to me. "It's not him," I say, though I'm not sure which one of us I'm really trying to convince. "This isn't him. Please don't hurt him."

Barnes nods. "Nobody is getting hurt while I'm around, including Victor," he says. "I'll be at his side the whole time. I promise."

I search his face and, seeing nothing but earnestness in his dark eyes, I pry my fingers off his sleeve and step into the hallway. But even with that reassurance ringing in my ears as the door shuts me in the hallway alone, I cannot help but feel like a failure because it should be me at Victor's side.

* * *

I ride out my anxiety locked in a bathroom stall. Mara comes in to check on me at one point, but I only snap at her to leave me alone. I stay until the tears have stopped and I can control my breathing. Then I clean up my splotchy face as best as I can at the sink, pause to study the ugly blue bruises blossoming around my neck, and walk out.

Dr. Wright is waiting for me outside. It's embarrassing to have her see me when I'm in a state like this. I respect Dr. Wright, and I want her to respect me too. I want her to think of me as strong and smart and capable, not puffy from tears after facing the consequences of my own foolish decision.

"Is Victor all right?" I ask before she can speak.

"Yes," Dr. Wright says. "But right now I'm concerned about you. Are *you* all right?"

"I'm fine," I say, but my voice comes out tight and whispery from my still-tight throat.

Dr. Wright purses her lips. "I personally selected and hired our security forces," she continues, meeting my gaze. "I know you've likely heard horror stories about what has happened in this facility in the past, but things are different now. Everyone who works here is someone I trust. I hope that in the future you won't hesitate to rely on them when you need to."

I choke down my emotions. It feels like adding insult to injury, to be reprimanded like this after the day I have had. But Dr. Wright seems to recognize that as well, because her expression softens. "But I admire you for your dedication to your subject," she says. "I'm not saying you did anything wrong today. Mistakes were made all around. We should've anticipated Victor's needs better and had a protocol in place for a situation like this."

"Can I see him?" I ask.

She hesitates. Her expression is regretful, and I already anticipate her response. "Let's talk in my office, Ms. Sullivan."

As I follow her down the hallway, a numbness settles over me. I wonder if this is it for me, if I'm going to be fired, or at least moved to another subject. The thought hurts more than it should.

Chapter Eleven

I'm not sure what to expect as I sink into a chair across from Dr. Wright and fold my hands in my lap. My heart begins to race despite my attempts to stay calm. What if I end up getting framed for this? What if I'm forced to take the blame? If they say it was my fault for getting too close to Victor, or for not ensuring that his restraints were secure, or for insisting on keeping the security forces out of the room during our sessions...

While I'm busy preemptively forming a defense, the door opens behind me. Director Ramsey steps in with a nod at both me and Dr. Wright before he takes a seat beside her.

"How is he?" I ask, my voice still a strained whisper.

"He is unharmed," Ramsey says, "and calming down now that he has eaten. The security team is also unharmed."

I sink down in my chair, feeling guilty that I didn't think to ask.

"I know you haven't been working here for long, but X-14 has never been violent with you before," Dr. Wright says. "Why now?"

I let out a small breath as I gather myself. At least I'm being given a chance to explain, rather than told that it's my fault. "I believe he was overcome with hunger. The diet he's been fed has not been tailored to his specific needs."

"Those needs being?" Dr. Wright chimes in, head tilted as she looks at me.

"Raw meat," I say in the pained whisper that is the best I can manage. "With a preference for human flesh, I expect." It's the only thing that makes sense. He must have been ashamed. Otherwise, why not admit to it before it got this bad?

Dr. Wright and the director exchange a glance. Neither of them look particularly surprised, more like they're trying to figure out how they're going to solve a problem.

"I see," Dr. Wright is the one who answers. "His previous meals were not kept on record... I suppose we now know why. Thank you for informing us, and for your courage in the lab today. As for you continuing to work with Subject X-14—"

"I *must* continue my work with him," I insist, managing to raise my voice although it hurts to do so. The rawness in my throat reminds me of the feeling of Victor's fingers gripping my neck, but I push away the thought. "I believe I'm on the right track, and he's beginning to trust me."

Dr. Wright's brow furrows. "You aren't afraid of him after what happened today?"

"He wasn't himself. It was a failure in his treatment plan. I should have seen the signs of the hunger before it became a crisis like this." Genuine guilt gnaws at me as I think of his recent irritation and mood swings. "It won't happen again."

Dr. Wright frowns. "Ms. Sullivan, we know *you're* not at fault for any of this. We're merely concerned about your well-being."

"I'm fine." The words are automatic. I haven't even had time to process this enough to determine whether or not they're true. "This was a road bump, but we'll overcome it. I believe I'm making progress with Vic—with X-14."

There's silence for a few moments. My gaze drops to the floor. I can't help but feel like they're judging me. Maybe I'm not reacting to this like a normal person would. Maybe I should pretend to be more shaken up, more reluctant to walk into that room with Victor again. But I've never been much of a liar.

"I admire your passion for your work," Dr. Wright says, and my head jerks up in surprise. "But I'm going to have to insist that you take some time off to heal."

Time off is the last thing I want right now. It'd be better to throw myself into my work until I forget all of this. My stomach lurches as I think about being alone in my apartment again, all of those empty hours, just like when I dropped out of school... "I don't see why that's necessary. I'm ready to get back to work."

"Take the week, Ms. Sullivan, and get that throat checked out. I insist." Dr. Wright gives me a look that makes my argument shrivel in my throat. "I believe X-14 could use the break as well. And we'll need to monitor his condition and mental state, make sure he's stable enough before we send you back in there. This is for the best, for both of you." She slides a folder across the desk to me. "And one more thing. We don't normally allow this, but I'd like to send you home with a copy of X-14's file. I'm going to have to insist that you read it now."

I sigh. Even that little push of air hurts my throat. Maybe she has a point. I glance at the director to gauge his take on this, but he only nods when he catches me looking. It makes me reconsider what the dynamic here is; he seems to be taking his cues from Dr. Wright.

I reluctantly agree and take the folder. As I stand to go, though, I pause with my hand on the door handle. "Please keep me updated on his condition."

"Understood, Ms. Sullivan," Dr. Wright says.

* * *

Days pass in a sluggish haze. I lose myself in watching bad medical dramas and arguing about them with people on the internet. I ignore Mara's texts checking in on me. I make some attempts at starting new taxidermy projects but always end up abandoning them a couple of hours in. The unfinished creations stare at me accusingly across the apartment, but I try to ignore their beady little eyes.

Finally, I have nothing to turn to but Victor's file. I make myself a cup of tea, curl up in bed, and pull it into my lap. I take a deep breath and open it.

Subject X-14: The Revenant.

The file is written in such clinical terms. Always "the subject" rather than a name, avoiding referring to Victor as *him*, as if even that could humanize him too much. And it's clear why as I read further. They didn't want to humanize him because then they would have to have a conscience about what they were doing to him.

These tests... My stomach churns with each new description. Even just seeing them laid out in objective, quantitative terms makes me ill. Weeks locked up without food or stimulation. So-called surgeries with no purpose other than taking him apart and putting him back together again, just to see if he would still work.

I think back to his surprise when I suggested using painkillers, how he told me that no one had even tried it before. They did all of this to him in the name of science, and they did not even *try* to make it bearable. There's no reason for it but cruelty.

I force myself to read the file from start to finish, even though my hands are shaking and I have to stop to wipe my eyes several times.

At first, I'm not sure why Dr. Wright insisted that I read this. There's no knowledge to be gained here. Even if there were snippets I could add to my notebook, I would refuse to benefit from this tome of horrors. But by the end, I think I understand. She's telling me about Victor's trauma so that I can understand him better, and maybe so I can continue to treat him gently. She's telling me to be different. It's especially important after what happened that I continue to think of him as a person, not a monster or a *thing*, as my predecessor clearly did.

But therein lies the danger as well. The reason I've been subconsciously avoiding reading this file. With these words weighing on me, it's impossible to ignore that I care about him as a person, not just a patient, even after the incident. I can no longer keep convincing myself that I'm being clinical about this.

And that is dangerous. I know what happens when I start to care too much; I know that pain is sure to follow.

But this time will be different. Different for me, and different for Victor. I will be nothing like the doctor whose name is signed on all of these foul excuses for experiments. That's the one thing I write down in my own notebook, so that I can ensure this so-called scientist has been punished as they deserve to be. A single name, underlined twice for emphasis: *Dr. Webster.*

Chapter Twelve

ven though I've been looking forward to this all week, my heart beats double-time as I walk through the MRF doors on Monday. I'm antsier than I thought I would be. I try to convince myself I'm just excited to get back to work, but I know that's not the full truth.

On the surface, everything seems the same as when I left it. The same faces greet me, the same white walls and tile await me when I walk through security. But my stomach ties itself in knots as I head down the hallway into the facility. Everything else may be the same, but after what happened, the relationship between me and X 14 will never be the same again. I'm not sure what he's going to be like after he hurt me, or what I'm going to feel when I see him. Will I ever be able to shake the fear that something like that could happen again?

I try to tell myself it could be a blessing in disguise. I was getting too close. Now I'll never make that mistake again. I'll never forget that he is both man and monster. Now, maybe, I'll have an easier time maintaining a necessary distance between us.

I take a deep breath, brush nonexistent dust off my clothes, and walk through the door.

Before going to work with Victor, I have a meeting scheduled with Dr. Wright. I walk into her office, set Victor's file on the desk, and sit without a word.

"Welcome back, Ms. Sullivan," she says, sliding the file into a drawer.

"Dr. Webster," I say, without preamble. "Tell me they faced consequences for what they did to him."

Dr. Wright leans back in her chair and gazes at me steadily, seeming unsurprised by my immediate launch into the topic. "So you read the file." I don't respond, and she sighs. "She was fired during the staff changeover I mentioned to you. I knew she was cruel, but I had no idea of the depth of her depravity until I was granted access to the files after her departure. X-14 was not the only patient she did irreparable harm to, but she had a particular interest in him. I regret that no one stepped in earlier."

"And after you realized?" I ask, unsatisfied by that. "You just let her walk away, knowing what she did?"

"We didn't have much of a choice," Dr. Wright says. "You know the delicate nature of our work here. It isn't as though we can call the police and explain the situation to them. There are very few government officials who even know the truth about what goes on here. We have to handle our own problems. And when faced between the decision to track down an errant scientist or focus on tending to the patients she hurt, we chose the latter."

It makes sense...but it still doesn't sit right with me. "It feels wrong," I murmur, "that she should face no consequences."

Dr. Wright meets my eyes and nods. "I know," she says. "But all we can do is focus on repairing the harm. That's why I brought you here, Ms. Sullivan. And that's why I am relieved you've chosen to continue working with X-14 after that incident."

"Of course I will," I say, and feel new resolve settle within me. "He's my patient." I fold my arms over my chest. "And while I have your ear, I have some requests as to his continued treatment."

* * *

Victor is waiting as he usually is, strapped to the table in the operation room with his mask on. His restraints have been reinforced and updated to include the fact his left arm is missing from the shoulder down. I can't help but be grateful for that. But there's a pang in my chest as I realize he's refusing to meet my eyes, staring at the ceiling instead. And the security guard standing in the corner of the room is a presence that is difficult to ignore, even though she remains silent.

I am relieved, however, to see that Dr. Wright already honored my request to get him some new clothes that don't resemble prison garb. He's wearing a pair of jeans and a dark V-neck today, rather than those awful orange rags.

"Good morning, Victor," I say, a thinly veiled attempt at normality.

"Morning." His voice is flat and unfeeling. He still doesn't look at me, nor use his usual moniker of *Doc*.

I bite the inside of my cheek as I put my gloves on. "How are you feeling?"

"Fine."

"Glad to hear it." God, this is awkward. I thought I wanted a more professional relationship, and I guess that's what this is, but it's painful. "I assume they've worked out the issue with your diet?"

"Yep."

"Good. Let's take a look at your fingers." This is fine, I tell myself. I can still do my job. Maybe I can even do it better. I give up on trying to make conversation and focus on my to-do list for the day. His broken fingers must have been set by someone else and are healing nicely, and fast. I bite back any questions and move on to conducting today's test.

We've now moved on to topical anesthetics, and I can't fight the way my stomach drops when I realize that'll require me to get close enough to touch him.

"Today's trial is a mixture of lidocaine and tetracaine in cream form," I say, fighting to keep my voice steady. I mix the solution and grab the swab to apply it. Once it's done, I have no excuse not to turn around and face Victor.

I'm trembling as I approach the table, but Victor closes his eyes, turns his head away, and remains perfectly still as I use the swab to apply the cream to his green skin.

He doesn't show any signs of the violence he displayed during our last encounter. Nor does he make any attempt at returning to what was once our normal. The room is icy with silence, aside from my occasional murmured question and his single-word answers. All the while, the security guard is there, hand resting conspicuously on the stun baton at her hip.

Today's test is another failure, another possibility crossed off the list. Victor doesn't look me in the face once during the entire session.

* * *

The next week passes in a blur. Every day is much of the same: I go in, I do my job while a security guard lurks in the corner, and I leave to spend a quiet evening at home.

I'm still trying to believe that it's for the best. There's no reason my strained relationship with my patient should affect my work. There's no reason why *I* should be feeling affected by the change in his demeanor toward me.

Loneliness is familiar to me. It should be comfortable by now. It *was* comfortable, before. It's not like Victor and I were ever anything close to friends; he was always my patient. Yet... I miss the way things were. The sense that things were easy between us.

Yet, though my usual method of coping with being alone is focusing on my school or work, I'm beginning to dread going in to the MRF.

Still, when Friday rolls around, I dread the weekend even more. The silence of my apartment feels oppressive. The taxidermy projects stare at me like even they are judging my solitude. I could keep my hands busy by starting another project tonight...but somehow it doesn't have as much appeal as usual. Maybe because I know it won't be enough to get my mind off Victor.

I sigh and dig my rarely used phone out of my pocket. With no small amount of trepidation, I open up my text messages and start to type.

* * *

"I'm really glad you reached out to me," Mara says the next morning over coffee.

She suggested a local place called Cup o' Happy, which is far too colorful for my tastes, but does know how to make a decent cup of tea. I sip it while eyeing Mara's whipped cream–topped abomination of a coffee across the table and try to think of what to say. I regretted sending that text last night the second she answered with a cheerful reply. I thought of canceling all morning while I got ready but decided it would be too embarrassing to back out last minute. It's just a coffee. I can handle it.

Except that I seem to have forgotten how to make small talk. Not that I was ever good at it. I forgot how awkward I can be because things were so easy with Victor…before the incident.

When a mangy-looking cat comes over and headbutts my leg to demand attention, I'm grateful for the distraction. I lean down to pet the creature behind its half-missing ear, and Mara's eyebrows shoot up.

"Wow, Schadenfreude actually likes you," she says. "He barely tolerates me."

My lips quirk up. "That's quite a name for a cat."

Satisfied, the cat wanders away, and I turn my attention back to Mara.

"How are you liking work at the MRF so far?" she asks. Then she cringes slightly. "Aside from…what happened, I mean."

"I like it." An easy answer, and a true one, but Mara's expectant smile seems to say she wants me to elaborate. I clear my throat, hands curling around my teacup and eyes on the table as I hesitantly say, "I'm suited to it, I think."

Mara nods like I've said something interesting. "Dr. Wright is good at finding people who do well here." She leans forward, eyes sparkling with curiosity. "What is it that drew her to you, do you think? It seems like everyone has something that makes them a bit...well...unusual, I guess you could say."

My mind flashes to med school, and I panic a little, words sticking in my throat. "Um..."

"Mine was that I started obsessively investigating the MRF," she says with a mischievous grin. "And also my interest in abnormal psychology."

"Taxidermy," I say, since I don't want to get into the med school business. "She said she saw my taxidermy."

"Really?" Mara's eyes go wide. For a second, I'm certain she's going to laugh, or wrinkle her nose in disgust, but instead she grins. "Can I see?"

I pull out my phone and pull up a few pictures. Her quiet *oohs* and *ahhs* of admiration at my more normal projects encourage me to show her one of my beloved creations, and she rewards me with a gasp.

"That's *adorable*," she says, staring at the rabbit with crow's wings with wide eyes.

A smile creeps onto my face. I'm pleased despite myself. This is the reaction I hope for and so rarely get. "Most people think they're creepy."

"Well, most people are boring. Your work is cute as hell, girl."

Still smiling, I slide my phone into my pocket. "Thanks."

"Sure." She leans back in her seat, and I do the same, a little more relaxed than before. "So... I know you can't say much about your work or your subject, but I heard some rumors about the incident last week."

And just like that, I'm fully tense again. "Mm-hm," I say, noncommittal.

"That must've been scary."

I raise a hand to touch my neck without thinking about it, and hastily lower it again when I realize she's watching. "It wasn't his fault." I don't know why I feel the need to defend him, but I do, especially when I think about rumors flying around the facility. "He lost control of himself."

She nods. "And I assume you've taken precautions so it won't happen again?"

"Of course," I say, thinking of the restraints and the mask. But there's a touch of sadness in remembering that I once hoped we would be able to remove them entirely for our sessions. I once wondered if he could be set free someday... But now, that seems like it will never be possible.

"And you understand why it happened this time?"

"Yes," I say, but it comes out a touch hesitant, and I'm sure Mara notices that as well. I frown down at my tea, thinking. I understand that his hunger got the better of him. But I still don't really understand how his hunger got to that point. And if I don't understand that, how can I truly be confident that it won't happen again?

"I've learned that trust is important in a relationship with a subject," Mara says. "If you no longer feel safe working with him—"

"He's my patient," I say, more sharply than I intended. "I'm not going to give up on him."

"Of course not. And I'm sure you're doing a brilliant job. But it's not a good situation for either of you if you're walking into that room afraid of him." She studies my face and softens her tone slightly. "Especially if he *knows* you're afraid of him. I know for Somnus, that would've been a big deal. He was used to everyone being scared of him. He would've been heartbroken if I was the same."

I sip my tea and consider that. I've assumed from Victor's

behavior that he was angry with me, but is it possible he's just...upset? Hurt? Guilty?

I let out a long, shaky breath and take a gulp of tea. "How do I fix it?" I ask, without quite looking Mara in the eyes. I barely know her, but I don't have anyone else to talk to about this.

She smiles, the expression sad but encouraging. "Tell me more about what happened."

* * *

On Monday, I march into work with a notebook full of fresh pages and new steel in my spine. Instead of asking a security guard to prep Victor and take him to the operation room, I enter the observation room I hardly ever use. I take a seat at the desk, set down my notebook, and hit the button to open the metal shutters on the viewing window, and another that will make me visible through it.

Victor glances up, clearly startled, from where he sits on the edge of his bed. I'm pleased to see that Dr. Wright has honored more of my requests to make his life easier, adding some books and new changes of clothes into his tiny cell.

"Good morning," I say through the intercom. It's strange, having this new barrier between us, but I can't deny that a part of me is relieved by it. It's hard to forget the feeling of his fingers on my throat, but I need to if we're going to be able to proceed. "Today we're going to talk."

Victor slowly lifts his head, brow furrowed, and looks at me through the window. "What?"

"We're going to talk about what happened."

He frowns, lowering his head again to stare at the floor. "No thanks."

"Fine, then. I'll talk and you can listen." I take a deep breath and look down at the notes I made after my talk with Mara. "First of all, I don't blame you for what happened."

"Stop."

I carry on despite his interruption. "I didn't leave to punish you, but because I was forced to take some time off—"

"Stop it, Lucy!" he shouts, and I flinch despite the glass between us, shutting my eyes. When I open them again, he's staring at me with a face of grim resignation. "There," he says. "That's the truth. You're scared of me. You're disgusted. As you should be."

I take a deep breath and straighten up in my chair. "That's not true."

"I don't blame you. I hurt you. I would've killed you if the restraints hadn't stopped me." His hand clenches into a fist at his side. "I requested a new doctor today."

Disbelief hits me like a bucket of ice water. "What?"

"It's for the best."

"That's not true!" I almost leap to my feet but suppress the urge. I try to calm my racing thoughts and heart so I can express myself properly. "If you feel that I'm not adequately meeting your needs, then I understand, but—"

"That's not what this is about."

"Then what?" I ask, my voice coming out in a whisper. "What is this about?"

He shakes his head slowly, not meeting my eyes again. "I can't hurt you again," he says.

"Then let's make sure it doesn't happen," I say. "Step one to ensuring that is talking about it. I need you to explain to me what happened."

He grimaces. "Is it not fucking obvious? I got hungry, like I always do. I lost control, like I always do. There's no fucking stopping it because this is what I am. This is what I was made to be. A monster."

My chest aches at the way he says it. It's not despair but *resignation* in his tone. As though this is some long-ago-reached conclusion that he doesn't have the energy to fight anymore. There is so much I want to say to him, to comfort him, but I don't know how. I'm no good at this kind of thing. But what I am good at is logic. "What's not obvious to me is how it got to that point," I say. "Why didn't you say something about your hunger earlier?"

He sighs. It takes a few seconds to answer, but I let the silence stretch out, refusing to give him an easy way out. "I thought I could handle it," he says. "The old staff used to bring me what I needed. Not often, but occasionally. Guess they didn't leave a memo explaining that." He swallows. "The new staff brought me animal meat. Which is...fine. Takes the edge off. It's never fully satisfying, but it's whatever. It's not like I'm gonna die of hunger. I don't *need* to eat."

I bite my tongue on that one; it's an issue to argue later. "And then over the weekend..." I prompt, since clearly something happened that made him change drastically.

"I was just...so fucking hungry." He grits his teeth. "So after I ate the meat they gave me, I tried to eat the other stuff they brought. Vegetables and shit. Didn't seem appetizing, but I thought maybe it'd fill my stomach. Instead, it made me sick. I threw everything up, and that just made me hungrier, so I...hit my threshold, I guess."

I'm quiet for a moment, processing that. "You should've told me." I can tell he feels guilty already, and I'm hesitant to rub salt in the wound by chastising him, but it needs to be said.

"It's not that easy," he snaps, bristling and defensive. Then he pauses and his expression falls. "I didn't want you to know if you didn't have to. I thought I could be stronger. I thought I didn't have to be...that."

"I'm your doctor," I say, though the words feel hollow. They're not what I want to say. I want to say *I care about you*; I want to say *trust me*. But neither of those things are appropriate. "I'm not here to judge you."

"Yeah. Well. You'd be the first." His lips curve in a mirthless smile that ends up closer to a grimace. "And it's not just you. It's everyone. This place." He glances pointedly at a camera in the corner of his cell, and I can't help but follow his gaze and wonder if someone is, indeed, watching us right now. I couldn't blame them, after what's happened. "You don't understand what it's been like. If I admitted that I was hungry, that I was having thoughts about eating *you*... They would've locked me in a cell and thrown away the key." He swallows, eyes shifting to the ceiling. "Again."

"Victor." I speak his name quietly and wait for him to look at me. "I understand that what you've been through has been horrible, and harder than I could ever imagine, but things are different now."

"How do you know?" he asks, an unfamiliar raw note in his voice. "How do you know it's not temporary? Or that one screw-up won't send me back to how it was before?"

"I know because you have me now," I tell him. "And I will always look out for your best interests. All I want to do is help you. But in order to do that, I need you to trust me. Do you think you can do that?"

He stares at me for a long moment. And then, slowly, he

turns his gaze away, looking up at the ceiling instead. "I don't know," he says.

I take a deep breath to try to quash the hurt that rises within me. I know this has nothing to do with me. These are old wounds, and it will take more than words to heal them. "All I ask is that you try." There's no point in trying to tell him that I care when I can *show* him. The best thing I can do right now is find a way to help him. "After lunch, we'll get back to testing."

Chapter Thirteen

I come into every session with Victor determined to fix things. I've decided that I've been approaching his care wrong. I've been obsessed with the solution to finding a painkiller to make his surgery possible and painless, which *is* important, but it's not the only aspect of his care. The hunger incident proved that there are other parts of his nature that I need to understand to ensure he's receiving proper treatment. The best way to do that—*and* to mend the broken relationship between us—is to gain a better understanding not just of his body, but of his mind. Of who he is.

In the morning, we test out painkillers, a security guard looking on from the corner. After my lunch break, he returns to his cell, I go into my observation room, and we talk. The glass is a new barrier between us, but it still feels more private, almost intimate, compared to the operation room where we're never alone anymore. And I get to see a new side of him this way, when he's not restrained to a table, but able to pace and gesture more normally. It feels like I'm finally getting to know him.

I'm not very good at this sort of thing, but it's easier when I approach it like research. I make a list of questions that I have about him and his background, and every day I pepper him with a few of them.

"Is it okay for me to call you Victor?"

"It's my name, isn't it?"

"Well, I wasn't sure..." I trail off, twirling my pen in my hand, but force myself to forge onward despite the discomfort of getting personal. "I wasn't sure if that was just the name that was given to you."

He pauses for a moment. "It is," he says. "But it's the only name I've got. I don't remember if I was called something else...before."

I nod and make a note of it. "How much do you remember about 'before'?"

He stands up and starts to pace the room, a nervous habit. Still, I sense that he wants to answer, so I wait patiently for him to continue. "I don't remember much. Bits and pieces. It all feels like stuff that happened to someone else."

"Hm." I write it down. "You remember different lives from different parts of you, or just one?"

"Just one."

"Can you give me some examples of what you remember?"

He winces without seeming to realize he's doing it. "I don't think I was a good person," he says. "I remember...running away. I think I was a foster kid. I remember sleeping on the streets, and...a switchblade in my hand. Sirens. Shoving money into a bag. Uh..." He pauses, and his expression softens slightly. "I remember...sitting on an overpass, watching the sun rise." His eyes become unfocused for a moment, lost in memory, but then snap back to mine as if he suddenly remembers I'm there and writing this down. "Just glimpses of things."

I record it all, dutifully and without comment. "Do you have any memory of how you died?"

He shakes his head. "No. Nothing. I just remember feeling cold, and then the next thing I knew, I was waking up."

"And what'd you wake up to?"

Something flits across his expression before it goes abruptly stony. "Her." He barely murmurs the word, but it is laden with such hatred that it takes my breath away. The look in his eyes reminds me of when he was overcome with hunger, but this time it's fury that renders him something inhuman. "My creator." He glances at me, and I school my expression into neutrality—trying to hide that, just for a moment, I was frightened of him, even through the glass. But from the intensity of his gaze, I suspect he noticed anyway. "Asking me a bunch of questions. Kind of like this."

"Right. Well." I bite the inside of my cheek. My instinct is to retreat from this subject. But this is what I wanted, isn't it? To understand him. As uncomfortable as it may be to speak about, his creator and his relationship with her is a core part of him. A part of him that I feel like I've barely managed to scratch the surface of. It's easier to be brave with this glass pane between us. "Did you ever ask her about your life before?"

He pauses for a few moments, nameless emotions flitting across his face; he seems to be deciding whether or not he wants to answer. "I did," he says finally. "She refused to tell me anything. I think she feared it might jar something loose in my memory. She wanted me to be a blank slate."

I nod and write it down, all too aware that I'm treading on uncertain terrain. "But you suspect she knew more than she let on."

"I know she did." His hand clenches at his side, and I shoot it a nervous glance, wondering if I've pushed too hard. Speaking about his creator brings out a side of him that I hardly recognize. His expression is cold, stony, but there's something haunted lurking in his eyes. "She had a file. I tried to steal it, once. It was the first time she...punished me."

I open my mouth and shut it again. I've pressed hard enough for today, I think. There's a cold anger in his expression that frightens me.

But I try to tell myself not to be a coward. Maybe it'll help to not end the session on *that* note. "Did you get your tattoos and piercings before or after you were resurrected?" I study an image of a snake that wraps around his bicep.

He blinks, clearly not expecting that question, and his expression becomes more familiar as he focuses on it. On me. On the present moment rather than his terrible past. "Before." He follows my gaze and turns his arm, studying a rose printed across his forearm. "Don't ask what they mean. If they had any significance, I don't remember."

I can't imagine what it must be like, walking around covered in reminders of a past that's lost to him. It makes my chest ache in sympathy, but the last thing I want is for him to think I'm pitying him, so I move on. "And the piercings?"

"I had the eyebrow and nose before, but the rest are from after." He sticks out his tongue to show the silver stud there, and then slides it back into his mouth with a small, sly smile. "Did it myself. Though I'm guessing you won't approve of that."

"I don't have to approve. It's your body." I scribble down notes about what he just told me. When I glance back up, he looks thoughtful.

"Yeah," he says. "Yeah. It is. The tattoos and piercings sort of remind me of that. I like the idea that I chose them for myself.

And despite the other changes, I kept them. No one can take them away."

I swallow, feeling a twinge of nerves. This is the part of being a doctor that I'm not good at. The *bedside manner* that was so often criticized in my schooling. It's never made sense to me; I'm not a therapist, I'm not here to understand peoples' minds, just their bodies. But, to my surprise, I feel like I've grown to know Victor during our time together. "That makes sense," I say. "A lot has been done to you without your permission. It must be satisfying to have a choice about your body."

"Yeah." He meets my eyes, and for once, I don't shy away from the contact. Maybe it's the barrier between us, but even after the incident, things are so much easier with Victor than they are with most people. His lips twist up in a lopsided half-smile. "And it means that I can have pieces of me that look almost...normal."

Normal. The word sends a shiver through me, especially with our gazes still locked together. I understand that all too well, the feeling I'll never be normal.

But Victor's differences are on the surface, not deep within, like my own. He doesn't have a chance to hide his from the world like I do. And instinctively, I hide again now. I hesitate, my eyes drop, and the moment of fragile connection snaps.

Chapter Fourteen

Our mornings in the operation room are oppressively silent. Victor rarely speaks at all, and I only do so to tell him what I'm doing as we do our daily tests. The security guard is a quiet but towering presence in the corner. It makes me feel strange, having a third person in the room; it also feels odd that the atmosphere is so different with someone here. I'm grateful to finish up our daily test—another failure—and go to the illusion of privacy in the observation room.

But today, as I sit down and open the shutters, Victor speaks before I can open my mouth.

"Today I wanna talk about you, Doc."

I freeze. "Hm?"

"You heard me. If you get to ask questions, so do I."

I take my time setting my notebook down and flipping through it so I can hide the array of emotions darting over my face. By the time I look back at him, I've controlled my expression. "My questions are for the purpose of your treatment. There's no reason you need to know more about me."

"Well, I'm not answering any more until you give me something."

I stare at him. He stares back, that twist to his mouth making him look effortlessly cheeky. He can be stubborn; I don't doubt that he's telling the truth.

"Fine," I say. I sit up straighter in my chair, hands clasped in my lap. He's right, it's only fair. "I'm not actually a doctor, for starters. I didn't finish med school."

"Why not?"

"I quit," I say, without batting an eye. I won't let him know this is a sensitive subject. "I wasn't a good fit for that line of work."

"Bullshit," he says. "You don't strike me as someone who would give up." He studies my face. I have the uncomfortable sensation that he can read every inch of me no matter how careful I am to keep my expression neutral. "So what happened?"

I consider what to tell him. "My classmates," I say. "I never fit in. And—"

"Bullshit," he says again, stopping me in my tracks. "That wouldn't stop you. You don't care what people think."

I suppress a nervous fidget. "You think you know me so well?"

"Well enough," he says. His eyes bore into me—one blue, one brown. "Tell me what really happened."

My gaze sinks down to my lap. I stare at my hands as my fingers twine and untwine. I shouldn't tell him anything. Especially not when I've never told anyone the full story.

I shouldn't. But I want to. And before I know what I'm saying, my mouth is opening and the words are coming out.

"I guess I should tell you why I wanted to be a doctor in the first place."

* * *

I became accustomed to loneliness at a very young age.

It was only my mom and me, growing up. My father was never in the picture. And my mom worked hard—she had to, to support us both. So she was hardly home.

Until she got sick. And then she was home all the time.

"I hate to admit it, but I liked it, at first," I say, staring down at my clenched hands in my lap. "Before I understood what it meant. Because she stayed home with me more and more often. She would read me stories and watch movies with me and run her fingers through my hair in a way I rarely remembered her doing before..." I trail off, lost for a moment in those memories. The two of us cuddled under a blanket on the couch, sharing a pint of ice cream. Mint chocolate chip was her favorite, and mine as well; I haven't been able to eat it since then. "And even when she got sicker, I liked that I could be helpful to her. I would fetch water when she asked, and learned to open her medicine bottles when her hands grew too shaky for her to do it herself. I liked taking care of her because I thought I was helping her get better." I pause, shift, sigh. Victor is silent, and I can't bring myself to look at him. "It took me years to realize that no matter what I did, she only became frailer. And even though I did everything I was supposed to, even though I tried so hard to help, one day far too soon, she was gone."

I thought I had known loneliness before. But that was until I truly had nobody.

"I was seventeen years old when she died," I say. "I could've gone to stay with a relative, but I barely knew any of them. So instead I chose to go off alone, to college. The money for school was my mother's goodbye gift. I wanted to make the most of it. I wanted to help others in the way I couldn't help her."

I lived my life around the goal of medical school. While others partied and dated and made friends in college, I studied, and studied, and studied. Taxidermy was the only hobby I indulged in, and only because I was able to justify it. It was practice, a way to make sure my hands were steady enough for surgery. Still, sometimes I felt guilty when I spent too much time on a project.

When I reached med school, it was much the same. I ignored my peers. I focused on the work. And I was good at it—most of it. There were some complaints about me being distant, cold, abrasive even. Still, I made it to clinical rotations. The finish line was so close.

"Then I met Ellie."

It's been so long since I spoke her name aloud. I whisper it now, like a secret, and my hands clench in my lap. I remember, in a flash, the first time that I saw her, smiling at me from her hospital bed. Her expression so bright and earnest for a girl who had been dealt such a terrible hand at life.

"She was young, and she was alone. Like I had always been. Except that she was in the hospital, and she was dying."

I try to state it matter-of-factly. But now, just like then, I can't seem to find a way to address it with my usual aloofness.

I was smarter than I was when I was a child, of course. I read Ellie's diagnosis and I knew what it meant. Unlike with my mother, I shouldn't have suffered from any delusions that I could save her if I worked hard enough, if I cared for her well enough.

And yet.

Ellie had no one else to vouch for her. I spent my lunch breaks in her room at her bedside. I stayed late almost every night so she wouldn't have to fall asleep alone. I scoured the internet and made far too many argumentative phone calls searching for alternative treatments, new clinical trials, anything that might make a difference.

"Even at her age, I think she saw the truth better than I did," I say. I feel like I've been talking for an impossibly long time, but Victor still hasn't spoken a word to interrupt me. All that I can do is carry the story through to its conclusion. "I think... I think she held on a little longer just for me, but she knew. She was just so young. She seemed so spirited no matter how much pain she was in. It felt like if anyone deserved a miracle, it would be her."

I clung to the delusion that she could get better until the day her small hand went limp in mine. I sat there at her bedside and I remembered watching my mother's eyes shut in the same way, and something inside of me snapped.

"I wanted to be a doctor because I wanted to help people," I say "But I realized that was just a delusion, like it had been with my mother. No matter how much love and care I poured into her, it never would've made a difference." I blink back the tears that threaten to spill over. "Being a doctor wouldn't be about saving people. It would just be accumulating a longer and longer list of goodbyes."

I thought if I was careful, I could keep myself separate from it; I thought I could stop myself from caring, but I was wrong.

And I realized I couldn't handle it.

* * *

When I finish telling the story, anxiety coils in my gut, embarrassment over sharing so much—with a patient, especially. I've never told that story before. I've never had anyone to listen.

Like I told him, I'm used to being alone. But that's no excuse for spilling my guts to a patient like this.

Victor is quiet in his room, sitting on his bed with his eyes on the floor.

"I guess that's why you like me," he says suddenly, taking me by surprise.

"Huh?"

"I won't die on you so easily."

I pause. "I suppose so," I say, aiming at lightheartedness. But judging from the look on his face, it's the wrong thing to say.

And somehow, as I close the shutters and lean back in my chair, I feel like we've taken another step backward.

Chapter Fifteen

Over the weekend, I end up staring at my notebook, feeling despair creep up on me. I may be making tiny steps of progress by getting to know Victor better, but I'm still not any closer to addressing the main problem of how to operate on him in a humane way. I had a long list of analgesic methods to test out on Victor, from topical to oral to intravenous. At this point, I've crossed them all off.

Not a single one has been effective. More than that, not a single one has seemed to do anything whatsoever to his nervous system. I still have little idea how his body perceives things. For now, I've accepted that many aspects of his nature are beyond my understanding; my time at the MRF has forced me to accept that there are things in the world that defy my conception of logic and science, and Victor's body is one of those things.

But it's one thing to accept that on a theoretical level, and another to accept that I can't accomplish what I came to the MRF to do: make surgery painless for him. Every day, I creep closer to resignation to what he's been telling me the whole time. What if it *is* impossible? I might have to take his word that he can tolerate the pain. He does have a weakened sense of it— or a higher tolerance?—so it won't be the same as performing a surgery on a living human with no painkillers.

Still, the thought makes my stomach twist. I was so certain I'd find a way. I wanted so badly to help him live without the pain he's grown so accustomed to. To show him that someone cared enough about him to do that, and prove I was different than everyone who had come before me. I asked him to place his trust and faith in me, and I failed. Every time I think of having to walk into the lab and explain to him that I'm giving up, I feel sick to my stomach.

I sigh, flipping through pages of my notebook featuring notes and lists and failed tests—along with the occasional sketch of Victor. His face in profile, the scars on his torso. All things I've convinced myself were for medical purposes, of course. But now, in the privacy of my apartment, I'm forced to admit that this has become more than a job to me. My curiosity, my dedication—they're not just about Victor's nature or his treatment. They're about him as a person.

In a way, he was right with his response to the story of why I dropped out. Subconsciously or not, at some point, I seem to have decided that he's someone safe to care for. Someone who won't leave me.

I keep telling myself that these stirring feelings won't affect my job. But now that I'm sitting here, looking through my notes, I can't help but wonder if they already have. Maybe if I could view this case more clinically, I would see more clearly. Maybe my feelings are holding me back. Every time I see another sketch of Victor, or a note about something personal about him that has nothing to do with the treatment plan, I wonder if I could've had a breakthrough while I was busy thinking about that.

I'm about ready to fling the notebook across the room in

frustration when I reach back to my notes from our first meeting. I remember placing my hands on his cool skin for the first time, gauging his reactions to the sensation, and wonder if I was already doomed at that point.

Then my mind stops. Reverses out of the hole of self-pity. There's an itch in my brain that tells me there's something more here, something I've missed. I force my racing thoughts to slow down, to take this one step at a time.

I've been approaching this from the perspective of nullifying Victor's pain. But as I've already noted, he isn't especially sensitive to pain. He *is*, however, sensitive to heat. Which means he might be sensitive to temperature in general...including cold.

Cryotherapy. Cold can have a numbing effect.

Excitement ripples through me. It's so simple. I didn't think of it because it's not something I would ever normally use in a surgical scenario. But this is no normal surgery, and Victor is no normal patient. It could work. It's worth a try, at the very least.

* * *

"We're going to try something a little different today."

Victor yawns. "Great."

Despite his lack of enthusiasm, I'm brimming with excitement as I unwrap the cooling spray. "Close your eyes, please." Once he does so, I draw closer. "Tell me when you feel something," I say, and apply the spray to a section of his forearm.

He braces, grimacing. "Cold."

"Mm-hm." I wait a moment and then prod at that section of

his arm with a gloved finger. He doesn't say anything. Holding my breath, I instead press on his bicep, which hasn't been sprayed. "Slight pressure on my arm," he says.

"And...now?" I touch the forearm where the spray was applied again.

"Am I supposed to feel something?" He opens his eyes, looks down, and blinks. "Huh. No. I don't feel that."

I break into a smile. "Really?"

He blinks again, and his eyes widen as he seems to realize the implications. "I don't feel anything except cold."

I run several more tests with the cooling spray, and each one returns the same result: *it's working.* The cold effectively numbs his skin.

"Okay," I say. I can still hardly believe it, but...I might have found a solution, or at least something that will help. "I think this could work. It won't knock you out for the surgery, of course. You'll still be conscious, and you may not have total loss of sensation, but it should help. If you want to keep looking for other methods, I can, but—"

"No," he says, blinking out of whatever reverie he was locked in. He meets my gaze. "No, I want to do it. This is better than I could've hoped for. I really—" He shakes his head, mouth twitching. "I didn't think you could do it, Lucy. But you did." For a moment, something flashes across his expression. He looks almost...sad. But then it passes, and I'm sure I misread it. "How soon can you operate?"

I take a deep breath, push down my nerves, and smile. "How does tomorrow sound?"

His lips twitch into an almost-smile, but then it fades just as quickly. "Yeah," he says quietly. "Okay." A pause. He clears his throat, and I wait patiently. "Just one thing. Do you think..."

His glance shifts to the security guard, ever-present and ever-silent in the corner, and back to me. "Will it be necessary to have the security guard there?"

I glance over at the man who's observing today, and back to Victor, who seems to be struggling to meet my eyes. It tugs at my heartstrings. Of course he must be nervous. It's a big operation, and I know how much related trauma he carries from his past. It's touching that he trusts me to do this at all.

I reach out and touch his arm, squeezing lightly. There's no hesitance in the motion; I've shaken off the nerves that gripped me after the incident. After the time we've spent talking, I suppose I've grown to trust him as well. Victor stares down at my hand for a long moment and finally looks me in the eyes. "I'll see what I can do," I promise quietly.

Chapter Sixteen

The morning of the surgery, I walk into the operation room full to the brim with nerves. As I requested, it's just the two of us today. The security guard will wait outside the room, at my insistence.

So today is the first time I'll be alone in a room with Victor since the incident. And possibly the last time as well, if the surgery goes smoothly—but I'm trying not to think about that.

I carefully unroll the full medical kit on the counter and make sure I have everything I need. Needle driver, tissue forceps, needle and thread, sterilization tools. The kit is stocked with anesthesia as well, though I won't be needing that. Plus, of course, the cooling spray.

Beside the kit sits a cooler with Victor's detached hand and forearm, both packed in ice. It's strange to see them, oddly clean stumps of flesh without any blood or scarring. It almost makes me wish I had been able to perform experiments on them before reattaching them, but no matter. This is the priority. I've made a promise to Victor, and I intend to keep it.

Even if that means I won't see him after today. I've been trying to ignore that thought, but again and again, it pops into my mine. Once this is over, I suspect Dr. Wright will move me on to seeing other subjects. New patients. He won't need me anymore.

It's such a selfish thing to think, but I can't help it. I'll miss him.

"I'm going to fix the stitches on your leg first," I say, trying to push all of those tangled emotions aside in favor of cool professionalism. "Then, if all goes well, I'll reattach your arm, and then your hand."

"Right." Victor stares at the ceiling, barely sparing me a glance. His jaw is set and his body is tense in his restraints, but I don't take it personally. He must be even more nervous about this surgery than I am.

"Please let me know if you experience any discomfort," I say. "You may want to close your eyes so you don't have to watch."

"I can handle it."

I pause. I almost want to reach out again, to try to comfort him, but today he seems closed off in a way he wasn't yesterday. Perhaps it's better to just get this over with as quickly as possible.

I move the sheet covering Victor to reveal his damaged left leg, with the stitches barely holding. I carefully snip through them and then apply the cooling spray. I test a few times to make sure he's numb and then grab the needle and thread.

Victor's eyes flicker to the tools, hovering there for a few moments before he pointedly turns his gaze up to the ceiling and braces himself.

I hold my breath as I first slide the needle through his skin—but Victor doesn't flinch. He doesn't react at all, still staring upward, his mouth a firm line.

I let out my breath and proceed, neatly suturing his leg back onto his body.

"My creator would take me apart and put me back together all the time," Victor says, surprising me. This is the first time he's initiated conversation about her, and I feel an odd spark of alarm. *Something's off.* But I ignore the feeling, burying it. I can't get distracted. I don't lift my eyes from my work, but I listen as well as I can. It's a distraction for me, but if it's one for him as well, then I can tolerate it. "Just to see how much my body could handle. Or for fun. I don't know."

I snip off the excess thread and lean back. I'm not sure what to say to that, so I focus on necessities. "Can you move your leg for me?" I ask. He does, hesitantly at first, and I smile beneath my medical mask. It worked. "Good. Thank you. I'm going to do your arm now."

Again: the numbing spray, the careful stitching, this time reattaching his shoulder to his left arm up to the wrist. I'm closer to his face for this one, but I still don't notice any change in his expression when the needle slides into his skin.

"She'd make me watch," he continues. Since I'm still watching his face, I notice the shift in his expression. Normally, whenever his creator comes up, he seems intensely angry. But now there's something different in his expression, something almost sad. Before I can interpret it, he turns his face away from me. "If I screamed, she'd sew my mouth shut."

I pause, struck for a moment by the horror of that image. I swallow hard, nausea stirring in my stomach. "I'm sorry." It seems like a worthless thing to say.

"For what? You didn't do it." He shakes his head.

"Stay still, please," I murmur, and return to my work.

"I don't know why I'm telling you this," he says after a moment. "I guess I just...want you to understand."

"Understand what?" I ask. But he only shuts his eyes and

doesn't respond.

I finish on the forearm and take a deep breath. "Okay. Last step." I turn back to the counter and freeze.

The cooler that held the hand is still there, unmoved. But the hand itself is gone. I blink down at it, uncomprehending. "What—"

The bed creaks behind me. I turn around, too confused to be frightened, and see Victor sitting up. Free of his restraints. At the end of the bed, the severed hand is dragging itself along, undoing the last strap on his ankle.

My blood runs cold as I see the expression on Victor's face: pure, cold determination. And then I see the syringe of unused sedative, stolen from my medical supplies, in his hand.

Victor cracks his neck and stands. "Sorry, Doc," he says, though he doesn't sound sorry. "Like I said, I hope you understand."

I barely have time to take a step back before he grabs me by the wrist and turns the syringe toward my neck. He's so strong—impossibly strong—that I know I have no hope of fighting him. I open my mouth to scream, but before I can make a sound, I feel the prick of a needle. I manage one deep breath before warmth floods my body and everything goes dark.

* * *

I wake up to a foul taste in the back of my dry mouth, a foggy head, and more darkness. It takes several seconds for my slow-moving thoughts to remember the situation. My stomach lurches as I realize I'm no longer in the MRF, but in the back of a moving car, lying flat on the seats with a blanket over me.

My car, I realize belatedly; I've never seen it from this angle before, and my vision is blurred with my glasses hanging from the tip of my nose.

My confusion solidifies into a deep, cold ball of dread in my stomach. Kidnapped. I've been kidnapped. And it's clear this wasn't a snap decision. All along, while I thought I was making a connection with Victor, he must have been preparing for this.

It's hard to force my sluggish brain to form a coherent thought. I try to keep my breathing even and move as little as possible as I carefully test my restraints. I'm bound at the wrists and ankles, and there's something over my mouth. Tape, it feels like. I didn't have that in my car, nor would Victor have access to it in the facility, so he must've stopped somewhere to buy it. He's changed his clothes too. Did he also get a weapon? I strain to see without alerting him to my presence. But all my eyes find is a severed green hand sitting atop the center console. When I look at it, it crawls over across to Victor's seat, scuttling like a spider, and taps him on the shoulder.

He glances back at me, and fear makes my body go cold.

"You're finally awake," he says. He speaks with the same nonchalant tone he always does, like this is just another day in the lab and he doesn't have me tied up in the back of my car. "I only used a fraction of the syringe, but that shit must've been strong." His voice has that quality of lazy indifference, like usual. But unlike usual, it sends a shiver up my spine.

He's been lying to me since the beginning. Getting me to let my guard down. He asked me not to have a security guard in the room, and I didn't question it for a moment. He's been planning this, and now it's gone perfectly for him. I can only guess at his intentions for me.

When the detached hand scuttles over to the backseat and

up over my restrained body, I tense and attempt to recoil. The closer it gets to my face, the more my heart pounds in my ears. But it only pauses to push my glasses up my nose, and then crawls back up to rest on Victor's shoulder.

"I'm not going to hurt you," Victor says. But it's not comforting—especially when he's lied so many times before—and I can't help but let out a whimper behind the tape. "I swear," he insists, glancing back again. "I needed a hostage. You were there. When I planned this, I never expected my new doctor would be so..." He trails off, lips pressing into a firm line, and turns his head back toward the road. "It doesn't matter. You'll be fine. I'll let you go as soon as it's safe."

Safe? I want to ask. *I'm not even safe from you!*

But with the tape over my mouth, there's no way to have a conversation, and he focuses on the road ahead without looking back at me again. The drug must still be in my system, because despite the fear gripping me, I soon find my eyes slipping closed, and I fall into darkness.

Chapter Seventeen

I drift in and out of consciousness during what feels like an impossibly long and uncomfortably silent drive. I should probably think of ways to escape, but my mind is still foggy from the drug and reeling from the shock of Victor's betrayal. When I am conscious, I can't stop myself from going over what he said again and again, thinking back on our conversations at the MRF and wondering how much of it was a lie.

When the car finally rolls to a stop, I jerk awake and tense up, uncertain of where we are or what's about to happen.

"Gas station," Victor says. "Need to fuel up. And get some food." He reaches back to pull the blanket up to cover me, but I squirm away.

"Don't make this harder than it has to be," he says, his expression darkening.

I mumble at him from behind the tape.

He eyes me.

I mumble more insistently.

He sighs as if I'm an inconvenience even though he was the one who *kidnapped me.* "I'll give you one chance," he says. "If you scream, the tape goes back on and stays on. Got it?"

Still glaring at him, I slowly dip my chin in a nod.

I remain where I am, tense but not recoiling from him, and he rips the tape off in one clean movement.

I hiss out a breath and then suck in a mouthful of air. I consider the pros and cons of screaming despite his warning and decide against it. For now. I don't know where I am and if it'll do much good. I need more information. Then, if he lets his guard down, I'll have a chance.

A shiver runs through me as I wonder if I'm echoing the thoughts he's had over the last few weeks.

I lick my lips, take a deep breath, and say in a slightly raspy voice, "I need to use the bathroom."

He rolls his eyes. "Sure you do," he mutters. "You expect me to let you walk off that easily?"

Even as my heart pounds, I arch an eyebrow at him. "Would you rather have me piss in your car? Because those are our options here."

He scowls. Gets out of the car and slams the door shut behind him. For a moment, I think he's just going to leave me, but then he yanks open the back door of the car and pulls me up to a seated position. He uses my car key to cut through the tape wrapped around my wrists and ankles and pulls me out.

My legs wobble, and I'm forced to hold on to his arm. He looks down at me, and I'm struck with the disconcerting realization that we're face-to-face on equal footing for the first time, without him in restraints. I didn't realize quite how tall he is compared to me; I have to crane my neck to look up at him.

The second I regain my footing, I push away from him and stand up straight, glancing around. It's still daytime, so the ride must not have been as long as it felt. I don't recognize anything around us, but the mountain ranges and expanse of desert suggest we're still in Arizona.

The nearby gas station is the only thing marking the area around us, aside from the road. It looks broken-down and dusty, the sort of place I'd be worried about entering the bathroom alone if I didn't have much bigger issues.

"Thank you," I say to Victor, stiffly polite. I start walking toward the gas station. But I barely make it a step before he grabs my wrist and pulls me back. I suppress a wince. My wrist is already raw from the tape.

If he notices my reaction, he doesn't show it; his grip stays hard and his eyes locked on mine. "Don't try anything," he says. "Don't talk to anyone."

"I understand."

"Do you?" His grip tightens, and this time I can't hide my flinch, but he doesn't relent. "I mean it, Lucy. You try to get anyone else involved in this, I will kill them."

He says it coldly enough to send a chill down my spine. I swallow hard as I stare up at his stony expression. I try to search for a sign of the vulnerable patient I thought I knew, but I can't find him. Maybe he was a lie the whole time.

I can't afford to assume he doesn't mean it. I barely know this man—this monster—in front of me. I don't know what he wants or why he kidnapped me. I definitely don't know what he's capable of. After a moment, I nod. "I'll be quick," I assure him, my voice quiet and subdued.

He studies my face a moment longer and then lets me go so he can pull up the hood of his jacket. I hurry into the gas station, rubbing at my wrist, while he follows at a leisurely pace. As I walk into the building, I flash the gas attendant a quick, tight smile. She gives me a bored look in response and then continues flipping through a magazine. She looks young, barely out of her teens, with badly dyed hair and a hoop through her nose, and any hope of finding help here quickly withers. I won't risk pulling her into this situation, and I doubt she's perceptive enough to figure out something is wrong on her own.

"Bathroom?" I ask, stepping up to the counter. The door jingles behind me as Victor walks in.

The clerk doesn't look up from her magazine. "You need to buy something."

"We will." I fight the urge to flinch as Victor stops behind me. The back of my neck prickles as he exhales cool air against my skin. "We're together."

The girl looks up, and her eyes widen. She gawks at Victor's green-tinged skin for a few seconds, until I clear my throat. Then she pulls out a key from under the counter and hands it over. I follow the sign to the bathroom, glancing back to see Victor perusing the beef jerky while the clerk tries to hide her stare.

She'll likely remember us if the MRF comes looking this way. But I'm not going to rely on that.

The bathroom has two stalls covered in graffiti, a single sink, and a tiny window. I do my business quickly—I *do* have to pee— and then eye the door while I wash my hands. I wish I could lock it from the inside, or that I had something to block it with, but no luck. I'll have to be fast.

I was being honest when I agreed not to tell anyone what's happening. I have no plans of risking someone else's life to save my own skin. But that doesn't mean I'm not going to try to get out of here. The window is small, but I think I can wriggle through. And maybe with a few minutes' head start, I can find a pay phone or something and contact the MRF. That's all I need: a few minutes.

I head back into the stall and use the toilet seat to boost myself up to the window. The crank to open it is rusty with disuse, but it still works when I put my weight on it and strain. Then I pull myself up and start to wiggle through.

It's a tight squeeze, and I'm probably going to end up toppling face-first into the asphalt below. Not a clean escape, but it's a way out. I squirm my way through inch by inch, forcing my shoulders through and wincing at the scrape of the edges across my skin. My shirt tears, but I keep going. My ribs and waist fit through, but then comes the biggest challenge: my hips... I stick tight and grimace. A deep breath, and I slowly move from side to side and start to feel myself slip through...

Then cold fingers close around my ankle and yank me back.

I shriek, bracing myself for impact with the floor, but instead Victor catches me easily with his one arm. He lowers me to the floor and pushes me up against the stall wall, forearm pressed to my throat to silence me.

"The clerk saw me come in here," he says. "We have about thirty seconds before she follows." His mismatched eyes are locked on mine and full of cold fury. "If she seems suspicious, I'll break her neck."

I try to speak. I can't, and my mind flashes to a memory of his fingers around my neck, the certainty he was going to kill me—but after a moment he eases the pressure on my throat. I gasp for air, trying to regain my composure as my legs tremble beneath me. He stares down at me, his jaw set. "What do you expect me to do?" I ask in a slightly raspy whisper.

"Come up with a cover story," he says. He leans his arm on the stall wall behind my head, towering over me with his face a few inches from mine. "Better be convincing."

I regain enough bravery to glower up at him. He won't kill me, I tell myself. He must've brought me along because he needs me, though I'm not sure why. But he doesn't need that gas station clerk alive. I can't risk her safety, so I'd better do as he says.

"Fine," I grumble. But if I'm going to do this, I'm not going to make it comfortable for him. I'll also make sure the clerk hears his name, in case the MRF or police are on my trail.

So I clench one hand into a fist and bang it against the stall wall behind me. Victor's brow furrows, and I say, loudly, "Oh, *yes*, Victor." I hold his gaze, my expression deadpan, though I feel a flicker of amusement watching his eyes widen in realization. "Please, harder! Yes, *yes*—" I keep it up, doing my very best over-the-top porn star impression. I hear the bathroom door open a few seconds later and then close again. I continue for a few seconds longer before trailing off. "There," I say. "Happy?"

Victor stares at me. He's so very close, his pupils suddenly so very large in his differently colored eyes. My breath quickens as I watch his Adam's apple bob with a hard swallow. I expected dark amusement in response to my performance, not *this*.

Then he pushes off the wall behind me, lets out a noncommittal "*hmm*," and steps back. I let out a long breath as I lean my head back against the wall.

"I still have to pee," I say loudly.

"Okay." He steps back, arms folded over his chest.

I glare at him. "Seriously? Don't be a pervert."

He rolls his eyes. "Trust me, that is not my thing. I'll turn my back."

"I still won't be able to go with you listening!"

"Try," he says, and turns around, still in the stall.

Cursing at myself, I yank my panties down and sit on the toilet. Of course, nothing happens. I wait a few seconds, hoping it's convincing enough, and then say, "I can't go with you listening!"

"This is fucking ridiculous," he grumbles.

"I'm serious, Victor. Just thirty seconds. Give me thirty seconds."

"Christ." He sighs and then leaves the stall. "Hurry the fuck up. I'll be waiting right outside."

I wait until I hear the door shut, and then wait a few seconds longer, listening. It seems like he really left. He must've truly been flustered. I didn't expect that, but I'm certainly not going to miss the opportunity it provides. I hop up on the toilet seat and go for the window again, squirming through the small space with a renewed vigor.

This situation has only confirmed it: I *have* to get away. Because Victor poses a danger in more ways than one. My feelings for him were complicated enough when he was my patient. I abjectly *refuse* to feel anything for the man who kidnapped me. I need to get free before I lose myself to this insanity.

After a few seconds, I manage to pull myself through the window, only to awkwardly topple toward the ground.

I hit the gravel hard on my hands and knees, stifling a small cry of pain. But despite the jolt of pain and the rocks digging into my skin, I feel a surge of triumph. I did it. I got away. Now I can run. Maybe not into the gas station; he'll be expecting that. To the road, then. Surely someone will stop for me, and all I need is a cell phone to call the MRF, and...

My thoughts grind to a halt as a shadow falls across me. I slowly lift my eyes from the ground, push my glasses up my nose, and glare up at the figure of Victor standing over me, blotting out the sun.

He tilts his head, regarding me impassively. "Seriously? It's like you're not even trying."

I scramble to my feet and bolt, running as fast as I can toward the nearest road. I barely make it a yard before he catches me around the waist. I yelp in surprise as my feet leave the ground and my vision flips upside-down. He throws me over his shoulder like a sack of potatoes, my head hanging down toward the asphalt, a sheet of red hair in front of my eyes.

"You—" I beat my fists uselessly against his back. "Put me down! I'm perfectly capable of walking."

"No can do," Victor says. The bastard is enjoying this, I can tell. "Because you've proved you're *perfectly capable* of running too."

I want to keep complaining, but I don't want to attract any attention. I'm still not sure if I believe him when he says he'll kill anyone who gets in his way, but it's not a risk I'm willing to take.

It's not that I don't want to get away. It's just that I'm not that desperate. Yet. He needs me, I'm sure of it, which means I have time.

So I hang there, limp and cranky, as he strolls back to the car. But when I realize he's opening the trunk instead of the backseat, I start wriggling anew.

"You've got no one to blame but yourself," he says, his tone calm as he drops me inside. A moment later, the trunk slams shut, and I'm trapped in the darkness.

Chapter Eighteen

I t's impossible to tell how much time passes. But eventually I find myself squinting into sunlight, a moment before Victor's tall form cuts in front of it. The sight of him makes my heart beat double-time as I remember my ill-fated escape attempt. Is he angry? Will he punish me? Have I only made things worse for myself? I don't know. I still have no idea who I'm dealing with here. I tense as he leans in and then holds a water bottle up to my lips.

I glare at him, but the allure of the water is too much to resist. Plus, I'm going to need my strength if I have another opportunity to escape. I open my mouth, and Victor attempts to give me some, but most of it spills down over my chin while I sputter. It's not that easy, drinking while lying down. He sighs, grabs me by the shoulder, and holds me upright while pouring water slowly into my mouth. He lets me drink about half of the bottle before taking it away.

"I need to eat," I say as he screws the top of the water back on. I eye him, taking in the clammy pallor of his skin and the more noticeable than usual shadows under his eyes. "And so do you."

His brow furrows as he looks down at me. "My needs are not

your concern."

"They are when you might eat *me* if you get hungry enough," I snap. It's a low blow, but right now I'm not feeling especially sensitive to his feelings.

A muscle in his cheek twitches as he clenches his jaw. He shoves me back onto my side and slams the trunk shut without bothering to tape my mouth shut again.

I run my tongue over my chapped lips and consider my options as the car roars along the road again. I could try calling for help the next time he stops somewhere, maybe even at a stoplight if I hear a car behind us... Perhaps even maneuver myself so I can kick out a tail light to alert them.

But I don't hear any sounds of cars on the road around us. And even if there were, I'm reluctant to drag anyone else into my escape plan when I'm not sure how dangerous Victor is. Plus, every failed escape attempt will only make him angrier and more wary. Maybe it's best to play along for a while, be a passive captive until I see a better opportunity to escape.

The car eventually stops. Goes again. Stops again. I'm straining to listen when the trunk pops open and Victor is standing over me. He grabs my shoulder and hoists me up into a sitting position, then shoves a sandwich into my face.

"Eat," he says.

"What is it?"

"What does it look like? A fucking sandwich."

I hesitate. It could be drugged. The water could've been, too, but I was too desperate for it to care. But Victor nudges the sandwich toward my mouth, and I decide it's not worth holding out. Whether I'm unconscious from drugs or weak from starvation, it'll hinder my chances either way. Better to continue my plan of playing nice until I see a good opportunity.

It's a little bit humiliating, eating out of Victor's hand, but I devour the sandwich in small bites until it's all gone. It tastes fantastic, despite the situation; I must really have been hungry.

"I hope you ate something too," I say. Then I wrinkle my nose. "And I hope you washed your hands before touching my sandwich."

He scowls and walks around the side of the car to rummage in the backseat. His absence gives me my first good look around. We're pulled over on the side of a highway, out in the middle of the desert. There's nothing but sand and cacti and distant mountains all around. No landmarks that I can use to guess where we are, just a whole lot of nothing.

My stomach lurches as I realize we're in the middle of nowhere, with no one around. It looks like a place where you would dispose of a body. Maybe I should've been more wary of that sandwich after all. Or maybe he's getting something to kill me with right now. But no—he could easily do it with his bare hands. Or his teeth. Maybe he's been saving his appetite just for this. Maybe he's getting plastic to wrap my bones in before he buries them, or...

...Or he's coming back with a container of beef jerky. He shows it to me before ripping it open, taking a handful, and shoving it into his mouth. "Happy?" he asks while chewing, glaring down at me.

I try not to look as relieved as I feel. "Far from it. But I suppose I'd rather be locked in a trunk than eaten."

"You *suppose*?" he asks, shoving more food into his mouth. Maybe I should be disgusted by the way he's stuffing his face like a starving man, but all I can see is the way the tension eases from his face and shoulders as he quells his hunger.

It's hard to relax. I know nothing will satisfy him like raw flesh will. But he chose to do this instead of taking a bite of me *or* finding a random stranger, so I cling to the hope he has something akin to a conscience despite this situation.

"Well, it's obviously not ideal," I say. "And it's not necessary. Where do you think I'm going to go?" I pointedly turn my head to look around. "Running out here would be a death sentence."

He finishes off the last of his meat, crumples the plastic, and tosses it to the side.

I give him a dour look. "Don't litter."

He shoots me a vicious smile. "Not exactly high on my list of crimes right now."

I only continue to glare at him. We're locked like that for a moment, until movement catches us both by surprise. We watch as Victor's detached hand scuttles across the ground, grabs the piece of garbage, and drags it over to Victor's shoes.

His smile falters. "God, you're a pain in the ass," he mutters—to one or both of us—and bends down to pick it up. He tosses the plastic into the trunk beside me and then slams it shut.

✳ ✳ ✳

After a while, adrenaline fades into exhausted numbness. My body is worn ragged from the effects of the drug and the long day. I doze on and off, barely aware of the passage of time with nothing but the dark trunk around me.

The next time it opens, I blink awake to the sight of a night sky and Victor's face. He's expressionless as he lifts me out of the trunk. I'm tense but I don't struggle; I know there's no point. Instead of heaving me over his shoulder again, he sets

125

me on my feet.

I scan the area as my eyes adjust. We're in a dimly lit parking lot outside of a motel. There's only one other beat-up truck in the parking lot, which may be broken down from the looks of it, and there are no sounds or sights of other vehicles on the road nearby.

We must still be out in the middle of nowhere. I doubt it will do me much good to scream or run. Even if I alert someone at the front desk, Victor will be able to take them out before they can reach real help.

Maybe Victor reads the intent in my eyes, or maybe he just knows as well as I do that any escape attempt here will be futile, because he doesn't bother with any further threats before he nudges me toward the motel. I study his face as we walk. He looks strained. Tired.

That's good. The more tired he is, the more likely he will be to make a mistake I can capitalize on.

But I'm tired too. Tired and sore and unsteady on my feet. I stumble on the way to a motel room, my knees weak beneath me. Victor pauses and then slips an arm around my shoulders to support some of my weight. I'm too tired to protest.

After glancing around to ensure there are no eyes on us, he unlocks the room and helps me inside before shutting it behind us. The room smells sour and stale, faintly damp in the way of cheap motels; I wouldn't be surprised if there were mold hiding in the corners of the nasty carpet, or perhaps in the shower. Still, the bed shoved against one peeling wall is the best thing I've ever seen. When Victor releases his grip on me, I practically collapse onto it.

My body screams with relief as I sink down onto the mattress, barely noticing the lumps and stains. But then I tense again and roll onto my back and lift myself up on my elbows as I realize what should've been immediately obvious. There's only one bed.

Cute in romance novels, not so cute when I'm trapped with the living corpse who used me as a hostage and kidnapped me.

Chapter Nineteen

When I turn to look at Victor, he's busy moving a chair in front of the locked door. He pushes it back against the wood and takes a seat in it, slouching back with a sigh. He sets down a duffel bag, and his detached hand crawls out.

When he looks up and meets my worried gaze across the room, Victor rolls his eyes.

"Come on," he says. "Give me some credit."

"You lost all credibility with me when you *threw me in the trunk*," I say.

"Oh, so not when I jabbed the needle into your neck and used you as a hostage?" he asks, tilting his head to one side.

I frown. "I—" I break away from his gaze, looking up at the ceiling instead. "If you had let me go after, I might've understood," I admit, even though it's embarrassing. "Even though you..." I swallow. I still haven't processed how or why I ended up in this situation yet, but one thing is clear. "You tricked me."

I know I should be scared of him. I should be angry. And I am both of those things...but more than that, I'm hurt. It's ridiculous, but... I told him things I had never told anyone.

It felt like we were starting to connect. Like I had found someone who, despite everything, matched my particular batch of strangeness. Now, I feel like an idiot for ever believing that could be true.

"I tricked everyone." He crosses one leg over the other and stifles a yawn, like he couldn't be more bored with this conversation. "Wasn't personal, Doc. I've been planning this for a long time. Couldn't let you get in the way, even though..." He trails off, and that mask of indifference flickers. Again I see that furrow of his brow, almost like he's regretful. But right now, I know better than to trust anything about this man.

"Even though what?" I ask, despite myself.

He meets my eyes. "Even though you were kind." He holds my gaze for a second and then looks down. "I didn't expect you to be kind. No one in that place has ever been kind to me. But it didn't matter. I had to get out. When I asked for a new doctor, I was rejected, so it had to be you."

Emotions roil in my stomach, but getting upset isn't going to help me. I remind myself of my goal: to get information out of him. The more I know, the more tools I have to aid me in my escape. "Why?" I ask. "What's your plan? Where are you going?"

He scrubs a hand across his face and chuckles. "What, you think I'm going to lay it all out in some supervillain monologue, just because you asked? Sorry, Doc. Nothin' you need to know that I haven't already told you."

"I don't understand," I say. "I know things were bad at the MRF before—"

He lets out a mirthless laugh. "Trust me when I say you will *never* understand what things were like there. They ran experiments on us for fun. And when they got bored, they'd lock us up in isolation for a few years just to see what would happen."

I hesitate, chastened. "Fine. You're right. I *don't* understand. But things are different now. Dr. Wright wouldn't allow any of that to happen again. She's working to change things."

"I'm sure she is," he says. "She and whatever that thing pretending to be Director Ramsey is." That statement is alarming enough to raise the hair on the back of my neck, but he continues without pause, "It's too bad they have no clue what they're dealing with in that place. It's a fuckin' mess. Otherwise, I never would've been able to escape."

I shake my head. "Still, I could've helped you. I would've helped you, if you had just been honest with me."

"What, help me escape? Oh, come off it. You would've been pissed about losing your favorite pet project."

That forces my gaze back to him. "Is that what you really think?"

In response, he reaches into the duffel bag and pulls out a familiar object, dangling it from two fingers: my notebook.

Heat crawls up my neck and spreads over my face as I think of everything written in there. The notes, the doodles. "Don't you dare—"

He flips it open to a random page with a lazy flick of his wrist.

"Victor..."

"Doc."

"That's *private*."

"I agree." He holds my gaze. "It's private information *about me*. You think I didn't notice you scribbling in this every time we talked? I felt so foolish when I realized. All of those questions were never about getting to know me. They were about *research*."

"That's not—" I choke on the last word, confused about whether he's right. After all, those are the same words I used to justify my actions to myself. "I wanted to understand you, Victor. Not because you were a lab rat, but because I wanted to help you."

"I finally understood your fascination with me when you told me that story about why you quit med school," he continues, as if I hadn't spoken. "I realized what I am to you."

"You're my—"

"I'm a project you don't have to worry about finishing, a toy that won't break."

I glare at him, unable to speak through the hurt and resentment I feel over him using my personal story as a weapon against me. "You're my patient," I say quietly. "No more and no less."

"Sure," he says. "A patient who won't die. Who won't leave. Who will always need you. You think that's any more noble?"

He holds my gaze until I drop mine, flushing with shame. Then he looks down at the notebook, and that shame only deepens. I have no words to defend myself.

He flips through the notebook, eyes scanning the pages, lips curling in amusement in something he reads. I flop back on the bed and put my hands over my face, unable to watch his reaction. The silence in the room thickens and boils, and I'm afraid to break it. I can't bear to look at him. Will he be angry? Contemptuous?

"You're very thorough," he says finally.

"It's what makes me good at my job," I say without lowering my hands.

"But this...this isn't something I told you."

After a moment, I lower my hands and look over. He's

holding out my notebook, the spine bent in a way that makes me cringe, to display a page with a single phrase scrawled across it: *Dr. Webster.*

"How do you know this name?" he asks, and there's something hard and terrifying in his expression that renders him almost a stranger to me for a moment. His anger is icy cold, and that only makes it more frightening. For a moment, it steals my breath away.

I've glimpsed that anger before when he spoke of his creator. But now it strikes me anew that there's no glass panel, no restraints, to protect me from him now. We are alone together without barriers, and I have no idea what he is capable of now that he's free.

Victor seems to mistake my fear for stubbornness. He grits his teeth and tosses the notebook onto the nearby desk. My eyes flick after it, and I resist a visceral shudder as it lands with the pages splayed facing downward. There's an odd, scurrying movement in the corner of my eye, and I blink as I see Victor's unattached hand crawl up onto the desk. It grabs the notebook and flips it shut, fixing the pages. It's not the first time I've seen the hand act in a way that seems to directly contradict Victor. How *strange*. I wonder...

Victor clears his throat and draws my attention back to him.

"Why am I here?" I ask, my voice a whisper.

"I needed a hostage," he says. "To get out of the MRF and to keep them off my trail."

My chest is tight. "And now? Surely I've done my part."

He shrugs, but the nonchalance doesn't quite ring true. "You might still be useful."

I don't know what kind of answer I was hoping for, but that doesn't satisfy me. *Useful.* So cold, so practical. As if I'm just a tool to him rather than a real person whose entire life has been upended by this. "I see."

"The MRF could still find us," he says, as if I had argued. "Or..." He sets his jaw, shrugs again. "I might need you to put me back together."

I blow out a breath that's almost, but not quite, a laugh. "Ah," I say. "Of course. And you still think I'll help you with that."

He finally lifts his eyes to mine again. "Were you under the impression I'm giving you a choice, Doc?" he asks, his voice soft but dangerous.

Right. Because he *is* dangerous. I don't know why I have to keep reminding myself of that, why I keep falling into the assumption that I'm safe with him, when he's given me no reason to believe that. It must be all the time we spent in the MRF giving me a false sense of security. But that was all a lie. The only time I saw the honest truth of him was when he was too hungry to fake it. *That* was the real him: those black eyes and snapping teeth, fingers digging into my skin, hard enough to bruise. I cannot let myself forget it.

I shouldn't be worrying about where this path leads for him. I have to focus on my own safety. My survival.

* * *

When I open my eyes again, I'm alone in bed with a shadow looming over me. My vision is blurred without my glasses, and for a moment I think it's Victor reaching for me, and my stomach drops in a way that isn't entirely fear. Then I register the huge size and unfamiliarity of the thing standing over me and shriek, yanking the sheets over my head in a childish, instinctive action.

"Lucy," a smooth, unfamiliar voice says. "My name is Somnus. We've met before. I come on behalf of Mara."

I slowly lower the covers and peek up at the shadow, squinting. This must be a dream, but normally in my dreams I can see without my glasses. But when I see the dark form again, and catch a whiff of smoke, I remember that secret room attached to Mara's office. "Is this real?"

"As real as a dream can be." That's an annoyingly vague answer. I open my mouth to press for more, but the shadow drifts closer, settling on the edge of my bed, and I clam up as I notice his huge, dark claws. "Listen. We are looking for you. Do you know where you are?"

"Um..." I try to focus despite the strangeness of the situation. Maybe this is just a dream, but maybe it's not; starting work at the MRF has thoroughly shaken my grasp of reality, so at this point I'm willing to believe just about anything. "I'm not sure. I was out for a while. Now we're in a motel somewhere, but he didn't let me see much." I rack my brain, trying to think of something helpful. "I believe we're still in Arizona."

The shadowy figure sits back, head cocked. "Are you hurt?"

"No," I say. "He doesn't seem to want to harm me. He needs me as a hostage."

"Good," the figure says. He sighs, a sound like wind rustling through trees. "I am sorry I could not stop X-14 from taking you. Nor can I reach him like I can you." He glances toward the door, and I see that Victor is still here, even in this dream. Slumped entirely still in his chair, head hanging down toward his chest, he really looks like a corpse. "His is the dark and dreamless slumber of the dead."

"Oh," I squeak, not quite sure what to say to that. "That's...

it's fine. I mean, I appreciate your efforts, but I don't believe I'm in any immediate danger. Don't worry about me." I pause, realizing that probably sounds insane. And suspicious. "I mean, do find me! Please. But..." I shake my head, not sure what I'm trying to say. No wonder, when I don't even know how to decipher my own feelings about this situation. "Please tell Mara that I'm okay, and I don't believe he intends to hurt me."

Even without any facial features that I can see through my blurred vision, I swear Somnus is giving me a skeptical look. But after a moment, he dips his chin in a nod.

"My reach is limited, so I may not be able to visit again," he says. "But know that we are looking."

Chapter Twenty

"Get up."

I wake slowly, confused for a moment about where I am and why my wrists are sore. But the moment I realize, I jolt upright, grabbing the covers and clutching them to my chest as if they'll provide any sort of defense. Victor is standing at the foot of the bed, a plastic bag in hand.

"I picked up clothes while you were out," he says, tossing it to me. "Change."

I catch the bag and glare at him. "I'm not going to change in front of you," I rasp as I reach for my glasses. I sound terrible, and probably look like it too. My mouth is dry, my head foggy—side effects of the heavy dosage of the drug he injected me with yesterday. That must be how I managed to sleep through him leaving and returning, a frustrating missed opportunity to escape.

Victor rolls his eyes but turns his back to me and starts to change without any qualms. I can't help but stare at the stitched-up, muscular expanse of his back. I've seen him naked before, of course, for medical reasons, but this is *different*. And it's different watching the way his muscles work as he pulls the shirt over his head.

I swallow, get out of bed, and peek at the clothes he bought for me. All black. I'm not surprised. It's not really my style, but I'm not in a spot to complain, so I pull on the sweater and skirt. The shirt is cut low, the skirt high on my thighs. I expect to cringe when I look in the mirror, but I'm surprised when I see myself. I look like a different person, but I actually look pretty good, aside from the wild tangle of my hair.

When I turn around, Victor is still facing away from me, fully dressed, hands in his pockets and shoulders slouched.

"Okay," I say, placing a hand on my hip. "You can turn around."

He does, slowly. He's dressed in a pair of dark jeans, heavy combat boots, and a gray hoodie. With the hood pulled up and his face shadowed, he looks almost normal at a glance. He looks me up and down, and his eyes darken.

"Looks like they fit," he says.

I try not to notice the way his eyes linger on my thighs. I shouldn't care how he looks at me so long as it's not *with intent to murder and/or eat.*

I clear my throat, fold my arms over my chest, and wait for him to look up; there's no guilt on his face, even as he pulls a roll of duct tape out of the pocket of his hoodie. I take a step back.

"That isn't necessary," I say.

But Victor's look is unsympathetic. "Don't make this hard."

"You're the one making this more difficult than it needs to be." I muster up a glare, even as my heart thumps in my ears. In all reality, I don't know what result pushing him will have. Maybe he'll back off, or maybe he'll step over the edge from being firm to being forceful with me. He could hurt me. "I got the message, Victor. If I step out of line, you hurt the people around me. I'm not going to risk that."

He takes a step toward me, his face so cold, it's barely recognizable. My heart hammers. I hit the wall as I step back again, and I'm surprised to see that he stops too rather than pinning me. Still, there's no softening in his gaze.

"Let me prove it to you," I blurt out.

"How." His voice is so flat, it's hardly a question.

"Well..." I swallow and try to take deep breaths to help me think clearly. "Let me sit in the front seat. It seems like we're in the middle of nowhere, anyway. Where am I going to go?"

He glowers at me, clearly expecting some kind of trick. I keep my expression carefully blank. After a few seconds, he sighs. "Fine. You get one shot."

I suppress a smile. One battle won.

A few minutes later, I'm sitting in the passenger seat, staring out the window while Victor drives. As I suspected, we're the only ones on this stretch of road, and there's nothing but desert around us. For a while, I try to scope out some kind of landmark or something that will give me a hint of our location, but it's all a blur of dust and cacti, and I don't know Arizona well enough to judge by the mountains in the distance.

It's certainly more comfortable than riding in the trunk, but the frigid silence between us is a whole different kind of discomfort. After nearly thirty minutes of stony silence, I clear my throat delicately and ask, "So, are you going to tell me what this is all about?"

Victor doesn't glance at me, his eyes remaining on the road. "You're smart. You haven't figured it out by now?"

I frown, rubbing my sore wrists as I consider my answer. I have to admit, a part of me was hoping he'd open up at least a little...but he's right. I think of his file, his hand gripping my notebook. *How do you know this name?*

"You're going after your creator," I say. "Dr. Webster."

His jaw clenches at the name. It's enough of an answer.

"But why?" That's the part I don't understand. "You're free now. You could go anywhere, do anything, and this is how you want to spend your life?"

"You say that like I have options."

"You *do*—"

"Looking like this?" he snarls, finally tearing his eyes off the empty road to glare at me. "Take a good fucking look at me, Lucy. You think I can live a normal life like this?" His lips twist into a horrible, humorless grin. "And this is me on a good day. You know what happens when I get hungry."

"That wasn't your fault," I whisper, even as my stomach does an uncomfortable nervous flip at the memory of his grip on my neck, his gnashing teeth.

"Stop saying that," he snaps. "It is my fault because it's *who I am*. What I am." He lets out a breath, shifting his eyes forward and loosening his death grip on the steering wheel. "What she made me to be. That's why I can never forgive her." His jaw sets, a tic jumping in his cheek.

"I read about the things she did to you—"

He scoffs. "So you think you understand? You don't. You can't."

"Still," I say. "Why give her any more of your effort? She can't give you any answers. She—"

"I don't need answers," Victor spits at me. "I need her dead."

I can't bring myself to tell him he's wrong to feel that way. And yet... "You don't have to let her define you," I say.

He shakes his head, his expression as flat and immovable as stone. "You don't know me, Lucy."

There's nothing to say to that. He's right. Looking at him now with that cold expression on his face, I don't think I know him at all.

* * *

Silence stretches out after that. Hours pass in a haze. I stay true to my word and don't make any trouble, just alternating between dozing fitfully in the passenger seat and staring out the window without really seeing the desert going past.

I try to form a plan. I am more certain than ever that I need to get away, for both of our sakes. Maybe I should keep focusing on my safety, but I know that if Victor continues on this warpath, he'll only get himself killed. I can't stop him on my own, though. Not when he's so set on this being the only way forward. There's only one choice for me: I need backup. I need the MRF.

Victor will hate me if I get him put behind bars again. The thought of him ending up strapped to that table with the metal mask on for the rest of his life makes me sick to my stomach, but it'll be worth it to save him. He can hate me all he wants as long as he's alive to do so. I'll find a way to be okay with it. It's the only way to save him from himself.

I've steeled my heart about what this will mean for him and me. But first I need to get away.

My troubled thoughts churn through my head, again and again, and I'm no closer to a solid plan by the time the sun sets. As I see the lights of a rest stop on the horizon, another thought occurs to me.

"We need to eat somewhere," I say, my voice quiet as it

breaks the long silence.

"Right." He turns into the exit lane. His lack of argument only makes me more worried about how worn down and hungry he must be.

I bite my lip. "We can stop somewhere other than a gas station, you know. That beef jerky can't be doing much to sate you."

"You think I'm stupid?" he asks, though there's no real bite behind it. He looks hollow, tired. "I'm not gonna give you another chance to—"

"Victor," I interrupt. "We both know that you being hungry can be a very big problem."

That stops him. His brow furrows.

"Look at this place. I have nowhere to run. I doubt anyone else will be here. We can both get a filling meal. Maybe not exactly what you're craving, I mean, but something better than beef jerky. Maybe a nice, juicy, rare steak." I watch his Adam's apple bob at the mere thought and feel a little thrill of victory. "I'll show you that I can behave without being tied up."

"Or I can just leave you in the trunk and get the meal myself," he says.

"I guess that works as well," I say.

He glances sideways at me, immediately suspicious at my easy agreement. "No," he says. "No. I'm better off keeping you where I can keep an eye on you."

I don my best poker face and inspect my fingernails. "Doesn't matter to me."

"Goddamn it," he grumbles, turning into the parking lot of what looks like a diner. "You're an idiot if you think I don't see that this is an obvious ploy. But you're right. I could use a meal." He stops the car and looks over at me. He leans slightly closer and says quietly, "Just remember, if you call any unwanted attention to us, I'll kill anyone who gets in our way."

I force myself not to lean back from him and meet his gaze steadily. "Got it," I say, my voice clipped. "Can we eat now?"

He gives me a tight-lipped smile. "Sure, Doc."

He gets out of the car. I do the same and wait for him to approach as a show of deference. The look he gives me is suspicious as he stops and takes me by the arm, pulling me close. "Behave," he murmurs, cold breath against my ear. Then he pulls a face mask out of his pocket and puts it on, hiding the torn side of his mouth.

I suppress a shiver. Instead, I smile sweetly, slip my arm through his, and let him lead me to the diner like we're a couple instead of a kidnapper and victim.

I'm not giving up, but I do need to be smart about how I play this. I'm not interested in getting anyone else hurt. And honestly? I don't need their help anyway. I'm going to outsmart Victor on my own.

Chapter Twenty-One

The diner is about what you'd expect from a restaurant in the middle of nowhere. Its classic, red-checkered tile is coated with desert dust. The door chimes behind us as we walk in, but no cheery waitstaff appears to greet us. The place is empty. We're left to select a table on our own. Victor leads me toward a booth in the corner, where he can keep an eye on the door and the rest of the diner without effort.

He slides into the red plastic booth. I move to take the seat across from him, but he wraps an arm around my waist and yanks me toward him so hard, I nearly fall into his lap. I let out an affronted huff, and when I look up at him, there's amusement glinting in his mismatched eyes.

"I want you close to me," he says, oozing false affection. "*Honey.*"

I give him an equally fake smile. "How sweet." I don't fight as he holds me against his side, his arm a vise around my waist. I play along by leaning my head against his shoulder and making myself comfortable. His threat is still ringing in my ears. I'm not sure if I believe he's capable of such a thing, but I'm not willing to risk it.

What bothers me is that even when I play out an escape in

my head, I still don't like the idea of him ending up in a cell again. I need to shake off this ridiculous attachment to the man who kidnapped me. This is exactly what he was aiming for when he got close to me over the past few months. He wove lies designed to get their hooks in me.

When the bored waitress comes to our table, we order: a rare steak for him, and a breakfast spread for me. She barely lifts her eyes off her notepad to look at us, and I relax when she turns her back. Victor looks fairly normal with his hood up and a mask covering the lower half of his face, but it's not exactly a foolproof disguise.

I glance around the diner. Looking for a phone, wondering if there's a back exit. Just in case the opportunity arises...

Victor wraps a strand of my hair around his finger and tugs, pulling my attention back to him. "Searching for a way out?" he asks in a low voice when I look at him.

"You caught me," I say, my voice tight. *He knows.*

He tugs on my hair again, not quite hard enough to hurt. His expression is almost playful. Might be endearing if he weren't holding me hostage. "I know you're smart, Doc. I'm not going to make the mistake of underestimating you."

"And I'm not going to make the mistake of trusting anything you say."

It's hard to read his expression under the mask, but he loosens his grip on my hair.

"You could've asked me for help, you know," I tell him, refusing to feel bad. "Instead of forcing me into it."

He searches my expression. "You really expect me to believe that you would've agreed?"

Yes, I want to scream. *I liked you, you idiot.*

Instead, I shrug and avert my eyes. "Guess you'll never

know."

He falls into a broody silence. Not sure why he thinks he has the right to sulk when I'm the one who's been used as a hostage and thrown in the trunk of my own car. I ignore him as best as I can when I'm still nestled against his side, and glance around the room again as I hear the chime of the door.

A couple walks in—both middle-aged, dressed in denim and boots, with the air of wholesome locals. They walk over and slide into the booth across from us. The woman soon excuses herself to go to the bathroom, while the man catches me looking at him. I glance away, not wanting to attract his attention, but I can still feel his eyes on me.

Our food arrives so quickly, I have a suspicion it came straight from the microwave, but I'm hungry enough not to care. I dig into my eggs and pancakes with a single-minded ferocity. The first bite only seems to make me hungrier as my stomach realizes that satisfaction is in sight.

I'm halfway through my meal when Victor mutters, "You little fucker."

I glance over and see that his detached hand has somehow snuck in with us and is trying to crawl over the table. Victor grabs it and shoves it into his sleeve.

I can't help but smirk. But then I notice that the man at the booth across from us is now staring. Did he notice the hand? Or Victor's face? He took off his mask to eat. His torn cheek is turned toward the window, but his green skin, his stitching, seem all too noticeable under the harsh fluorescent lights.

Panic sparks through my chest. Surely this man can't know that Victor is something other than human—he could have, I don't know, some extreme form of hypochromic anemia, or another rare disease—but still, this is attention we don't want.

As much as I want to get away from Victor, this is the kind of situation I definitely *don't* need. I can't get other people involved, especially not in public and in the middle of nowhere.

"Victor," I whisper, pressing against his neck.

"Don't need your help," he grumbles.

"I wasn't offering it," I hiss into his ear, hoping it looks like I'm whispering sweet nothings. "You're attracting attention."

The woman has returned to the man's booth, and he's whispering something to her. She's staring now too; it makes the back of my neck prickle with alarm.

Victor glances at them, and then back at his meal. "So?" he asks, but I feel his muscles tense through his hoodie. His good hand reaches for his steak knife, and his eyes stay turned in the couple's direction, narrowing with suspicion.

I'm stiff with tension too. Maybe that's what they're picking up on. That we look less like a couple and more like...well. Like a kidnapper and a victim. It terrifies me to think that *I* might be the one screwing this up and putting them in danger.

I think fast. No time to doubt myself. "Kiss me," I whisper in Victor's ear.

He jerks. "What?"

"Kiss me," I say again. No matter how nosy this couple is, they're probably not big enough creeps to stare at some obvious PDA. People's natural instinct is to turn away.

Victor slowly turns to look down at me. He hesitates, but I reach up to grab him by the jaw, covering the ripped side of his mouth with my palm. I tug him roughly down to me, and he finally leans in and presses his lips to mine.

Cold. It sends a zip of surprise up my spine. I shouldn't be startled—I've felt the coolness of his skin before—but it's still a shock to feel cold lips against mine. More unexpected still is his gentleness as he returns my kiss.

He kisses me slowly, his nose nudging mine, his thumb rubbing over my jaw. I kiss him back in the same way, sliding one hand into his hood to fist in his hair. He lets out a soft noise as I grip it perhaps harder than necessary.

Maybe he's trying to be a gentleman, or maybe he's just not into this, but this isn't about what we want right now. It's about putting on a good enough show to make people look away. So I scoot closer and throw a leg over his lap and sink my teeth into his lower lip. *Come on, Victor. Play along.*

He lets out a cold exhale against my mouth and kisses me harder. He nips at my lip; I feel the throb all the way down between my legs and stiffen in shock. But I don't stop kissing him. I can't, even though it frightens me that this is genuinely turning me on. His tongue coaxes my mouth open, his hand grips my thigh, and I hope he believes that the whimper I let out is all a part of the act.

I wish I could believe it myself. But fuck, he's good at this. It's like he knows exactly what I like.

We make out for a solid thirty seconds, practically devouring each other's mouth, before I stop and open my eyes. He's staring up at me through half-lidded eyes, his pupils blown wide. I'm breathing hard, all too aware of his hand still wrapped around my thigh, precariously close to finding the telltale dampness soaking through my panties. I swallow hard, pulling back, and sneak a glance over at the couple in the other booth. They're both very interested in their coffee.

We successfully put them off from staring, I think. Yet I find myself lingering on his lap a little longer, leaning in to press one last kiss to his nose before I slide away. I sit there all too aware of the aching of my core and the fact that nobody has made me feel this disastrously out of control in...ever.

I clear my throat and dig back into my food, doing my very best to act nonchalant. But it's hard when I feel Victor's eyes return to me time and time again, and I still feel the lingering sensation of his fingers on my thigh like it's branded there.

As I'm finishing up my meal, I notice, out of the corner of my eye, that the couple at the table across is staring our way again. Annoyance flickers through me. How nosy can two people be? Am I going to have to repeat our earlier performance? And why don't I hate the idea nearly as much as I should?

But as I slowly turn to face Victor again, I instead catch a glimpse of something behind him and realize that the couple isn't staring at us at all. They're staring at the hulking figure standing outside of the window with his dark eyes fixed on Victor.

Chapter Twenty-Two

My breath hitches. The man outside is *huge*, his proportions seemingly impossible with his bulging arms and barely there neck, and something about his odd, slouching posture calls Victor to mind. I have a distinct and terrifying notion that I'm looking at something not quite human, and something very dangerous.

"Victor," I whisper, and he turns to look just in time for the man—*creature*—to raise one giant scarred fist and slam it into the window.

As the glass shatters, time seems to move double; there's only a blur of movement and screams, and all of a sudden I'm on the diner floor. I sit up and hear the crunch of glass beneath me through the ringing in my ears. I distantly think that I'm lucky I wasn't hurt, and then I lift my trembling hand to push my glasses up my nose and see blood.

Shock. I'm in shock. I can't even tell how badly I'm hurt because the adrenaline pulsing through my body makes it impossible to feel anything but numbness. Still, my first thought is—

"Victor?"

He was sitting between me and the window. He would've

taken the brunt of the force. I have a distant notion that he may have shoved me to the floor to shield me. But he's not here now. A man bends to help me up, but it's the denim-dressed stranger who stared at us earlier, not Victor.

"Where... Where...?" I can't seem to form a coherent question. My body is shaking. The stranger puts an arm around me to steady me as my knees go weak, saying something that's probably intended to be comforting, but I can't seem to make sense of the words. Instead, I turn to look at the jagged-edged hole where the window once was, and the booth where we were sitting—now holding only Victor's detached hand, twitching on its back like an overturned spider.

And then my eyes move to the parking lot beyond. My heart surges as I finally see Victor outside, and then it sinks again as I realize he's out there with the creature, grappling with it. Because of course he is. Of course when danger came, he ran toward it instead of away. Never mind that he was leaving me behind, dazed and covered in broken glass.

But God, what an idiot I am, because instead of taking this opportunity to run, to call the MRF, I find myself shaking free of the stranger's grip and running for the door, driven by concern for *Victor*.

That thing outside is huge, and he's not ready to face it. He's still missing a hand, he has no *chance*—

Yet right now, it's the hulking creature that's fleeing into a car, while Victor gives chase. As the door shuts, Victor flings himself against the vehicle like a rabid animal, shouting something. He doesn't back off even as the car roars to life and reverses, the bumper clipping him in the hip and sending him sprawling to the asphalt.

"*Victor!*" I scream again, running to him.

He looks up at me and he's *grinning*, a wide feral grin, even though his lower body is twisted at a sickening angle. He reaches down and yanks his hip back into place with a sick crunch. When he stands, he's still a little sideways, his lower half not turned at the same angle as the upper. Yet, judging from the manic gleam in his eyes, he doesn't even notice.

"That was a warning," he crows. "Because I'm getting close." He throws back his head and laughs. "She basically confirmed her location! Still in the same goddamn place. The MRF must've called her, and then the idiot, she..." Finally, his eyes light on me, and he blinks and seems to actually see me. His brow furrows. "Lucy," he says.

I follow his gaze downward and see the thick, jagged shard of glass sticking out of my bicep. I still can't feel anything, so I just blink, trying to make sense of it. "Oh," I whisper, and my vision goes white.

* * *

I wake to the hot sting of pain and lash out instinctively. But strong, cold fingers grip my arms and hold me down, rendering me entirely incapable of moving with hardly the slightest amount of pressure.

"Stay still, Lucy. It's my turn to be the doctor."

I hiss out a breath as my arm continues to throb. But not just my arm. There are little sparks of pain all over my body, a sharp twinge like paper cuts but much worse. I finally focus. We're in another motel room, slightly less grimy than the last one, and Victor is sitting on the edge of the bed where I'm sprawled.

"Do you know what you're doing?" I ask, though I stay still

as he releases me. He has a medical kit open on his lap. *My medical kit.* He must've stolen it from the MRF along with me.

"I've been stitching myself up for years."

"Yes, but I'm not a *walking corpse*," I snap.

A flash of hurt crosses his face. I relish it. I want him to hurt, because *I'm* hurting, and not just physically, as memories of the incident rush in.

"Fine." He sets the medical kit beside me and stands. "You can take care of yourself, then."

"No surprise there," I mutter, sitting up and grabbing the supplies. I can't even bring myself to look at him as a hot pit of anger simmers in my stomach.

"What's that supposed to mean?" he snaps. "I pushed you to safety, Lucy. And then I carried you here and took care of you."

"Yes, and you *left me*," I snap at him. "You left me on the floor, covered in broken glass. You didn't even notice I was hurt. And I didn't even notice it either, because I was too worried about you throwing yourself into more danger like an *idiot*."

As the silence stretches, I finally lift my eyes to glare at him and find him staring at me.

"Are you mad about me putting *you* in danger or me putting *myself* in danger?" he asks.

"All of it." I shake my head in frustration, trying to focus on the first aid supplies again and the cuts on my arm. The shard in my arm has already been removed, and it's neatly bandaged. The rest of the smaller cuts on my arms and hands have been cleaned and still sting of antiseptic. The wounds are all shallow.

But I'm still shockingly aware of how much worse it could've been. If that piece of glass had gone through my hand instead of my arm, it would've ended my surgical career. My taxidermy.

All of it. Everything I love could've been taken from me in one cruel twist of fate.

And instead of preventing further damage, I chased after a man who didn't even pause to check if I was okay before flinging himself at a moving car. What was I thinking?

I'm mad at Victor, yes, but I'm also mad at myself. For choosing his safety above my own when he clearly doesn't give a shit about *either* of our lives. I could've found a phone, called the MRF, and ended this. But I was too weak.

"I don't know what to tell you. Both of us are fine, so—"

I raise my hand to wipe at the tears welling in my eyes, and Victor stops as he notices.

"Lucy," he says, more gently. "Hey. You're fine. It wasn't as bad as it looked." He reaches for me, but I jerk away.

"Don't *touch* me," I snap at him, even as hot tears spill over and blur my vision. "This is all your fault! All of it!"

Damn him for making me feel like this. Damn me for being stupid enough to care even after he's shown me, again and again, that I'm nothing but a tool for him. Victor doesn't care about anything, least of all me, except for the fact that I'm useful to getting him closer to his revenge.

How did I let myself get in this deep? He lied to me, kidnapped me, and now he left me behind without a second thought. I'm a fool to even be hurt at this point.

"You told me one day I'd see you as you are," I whisper. "Well, you were right. I see you, Victor."

This is why I hold people at arm's length. I've always known that relationships lead to pain. So why, oh why, did I choose *him* to let through my walls?

He pulls away from me as I gulp down a sob, trying to get a hold of myself.

"I'll give you some space," he says. He turns and walks out the door, slamming it behind him.

Chapter Twenty-Three

I sit on the bed until my tears run dry. The thought of trying to escape crossed my mind, but even after stomping out like a child, Victor left his detached hand clinging to the doorknob so he'd undoubtedly know if I tried anything.

"Fuck you," I whisper at the hand, sniffling to myself. It does not respond.

Once I'm done with *that* tantrum, I wipe my tears, clean my glasses, and force myself to think. I could try to run now, but I don't know where Victor is. And I'm not just trying to get away for my own sake. He's a danger to himself and others. I cannot let myself be distracted by any meaningless worries about whether or not contacting the MRF is the right thing to do; it is the *only* thing I can do, for both my safety and his.

I blew my opportunity in the diner. But maybe the fact I didn't run was enough to get him to let his guard down.

So I think: what do I know about Victor? What information have I gained that I can use against him?

As hectic as the diner situation was, I did solidify one important fact before the creature showed up: Victor is attracted to me. If I wasn't sure before, I am now, after the way he reacted to my kiss.

I'm not a femme fatale, but... I'm no innocent, either.

I force myself out of bed and into the bathroom, where I shed my bloodstained clothes. I don't have anything else to wear, but there is the thin hotel robe. I put it on over just my underwear and then stare at myself in the mirror. The pale pink fabric is nearly sheer, so thin that my nipples and panty line are visible through it. The idea of being seen like this makes me blush, but perhaps it will get the job done.

And my bandaged upper arm, visible through the sheer robe, is a reminder of why I *need* to do this. I wash my face, finger-comb my hair, and then climb back into bed and wait for Victor to return.

It takes an hour for him to appear. When he does, he's carrying a plastic bag. His shoulders are slumped, and the bags under his eyes look deeper. I wonder if he's getting hungrier, without access to human flesh, and it gives me a new shiver of fear about what I intend to do.

But there's no turning back. I need to stop making excuses.

Victor's expression shifts as he looks at me. He seems almost surprised. I wonder, then, if leaving me alone was intentional, if guilt drove him to give me a chance to get away. But then he notices the bathrobe I'm wearing, and his eyes widen and linger for an entirely different reason.

I flush, suddenly feeling foolish. "There was nothing else to wear," I say defensively, even though he hasn't spoken yet.

"Right," he says, shaking his head. "I should...go get fresh clothes. But I did get this." He takes out a variety of medical supplies. "To restock your kit."

"Good," I say. "Because I was thinking I should take a look at your stitches. And maybe get your hand reattached."

"I got this for you," he says. "You don't have to—"

"I know," I say. "But I realized... If you're really going to do this, then I, um..." God, I'm no good at deception. I swallow and push my hair behind my ear. "I want you to have the best chance possible of success," I say. "Let me look after you, Victor."

I see the effect it has on him, the way his features soften. I hate myself for deceiving him, but I press on.

"Missing a hand will make you easier to identify. It earned us too much attention today." His brow quirks further upward at the use of *us*, and I curse myself. I'm not on his side. I'm *not*. But him getting caught in a public place like that simply has too many variables that could lead to disaster. It wouldn't be good for either one of us. "People will remember you if they see you. And..." I pause, nibbling my lip, hating that I'm genuinely concerned about his well-being even though he's holding me captive. "When you fight your creator, you'll need to be in the best shape you can be. Right?" If the MRF doesn't get here before he takes off, I'll be comforted by the fact he's fixed up.

He eyes me and then lets out a huff of a laugh. "You really think I'm gonna believe that? You're just trying to get a weapon in your hands."

"We both know it's not going to do me any good," I say. "You could break my spine with one hand. I'm no threat to you, even with a scalpel."

He stares at me a few moments longer, clear disbelief in his eyes, but then he shrugs. "I am getting tired of carrying the damn thing around," he says. He looks over at the hand—currently sitting on the edge of the TV stand—and reaches for it.

But it scuttles away with surprisingly deft fingers. Victor scowls, grabs for it again, and catches it this time. He holds it up by the palm as it wriggles. He stares at it; it flips him off, upside-down. I have the sense some kind of stand-off is occurring. A moment later, Victor lets out a sound that's half laugh, half groan, and tosses the hand back on the bed. "Whatever," he says, turning back to me. "Don't bother with the hand. Damn thing's got a mind of its own. And I guess it prefers it that way."

My mouth opens and shuts again. I'm not sure how to feel about Victor being willing to give up his own hand because it...wants to be unattached? It's rather absurd. And surprising that he'd go along with it. But perhaps it shouldn't be. Victor was never given any choice in what happened to his body. I should try to convince him to let me do the surgery, for this to go as planned, yet I can't seem to bring myself to.

"But my leg is pretty fucked up," he continues when I don't comment. "You can fix that." He tosses the medical kit on the bed with me. I slowly scoot forward and open it, eyeing the medical tools at my disposal. Scissors and scalpels and thread to stitch him up with.

I pick up the scalpel and take a deep breath. Then I turn to Victor.

"Sit down."

He takes a seat on a chair. I walk over, scalpel in hand. He tenses, his eyes on the potential weapon—but then I slowly sink to my knees on the carpet in front of him. Victor's eyebrows shoot up before he controls his expression.

"What are you doing, Lucy?" he asks, his voice even lower and more gravelly than normal.

"Fixing your leg, like you said," I tell him, like I don't know exactly what I'm doing looking up from my knees in a bathrobe like this. I feel a rush of self-consciousness that he'll find this ridiculous rather than enticing, but then I brush my hair over my shoulder and notice the way his eyes track my every move. He's exactly what I want him to be: distracted.

"Your hips look misaligned too," I say. Which is not very sexy, but I follow it up by nibbling my lip and then asking, "Could you take off your pants for me?"

He considers it and then undoes his belt. His zipper. He slides his pants down his legs and pushes them aside, leaving him wearing only boxer briefs on his lower half. There's a noticeable bulge *very* close to my eye level, but I try to focus on the stitching instead. One leg—the one I restitched at the MRF—looks fine; the new sutures held. The other one is not so lucky after his run-in with the car. "I'm going to cut the remaining stitches here and redo them, if that's all right."

I pause, glancing up at him. His pupils are huge, his eyes locked on mine. He blinks for a moment before registering what I want.

"Yes."

I suppress a shiver at the throaty quality in his voice and try to focus on the task at hand instead of the fact I'm on my knees in front of him. I planned this to get him to let his guard down, but he's not the only one who's distracted. I shouldn't be affected by the way he leans back in his chair in a languid slouch, the way his legs are spread so I am kneeling between them, the fact he's obviously hard. I shouldn't be thinking of it at all. I should be thinking of *escaping*.

I certainly shouldn't be getting turned on by being on my knees in the hotel room for my kidnapper. My bathrobe feels so thin on my skin that I might as well be naked.

I bite the inside of my cheek, hoping my embarrassment isn't as obvious as it feels. I force myself to focus. As I cut through the stitches on his leg, I consider that I could leave him this way and run. But if he managed to crawl to the car and escape, to go after his creator anyway, I would never be able to live with myself.

There will be a better chance.

I rotate Victor's leg into the proper position and pick up the needle and thread from the kit. I glance up at Victor as I do so, and make sure his eyes are locked with mine as I slide the scalpel into the sleeve of the robe. His eyes are darker than normal, his pupils enormous as they watch me.

I break eye contact and suck in a breath. This time it's from nerves as I realize what I'm about to do. This may be part of an escape plan, but I still don't want to botch the surgery, because try as I might, I can't seem to hate Victor.

"All of that work, and I'm going to have to do this with no painkiller anyway," I whisper, trying to break the tension.

"Hit me with your worst, Doc," he drawls, and somehow it sounds like a come-on with his voice this low.

"If I didn't know any better, I'd say you were enjoying this," I say as I gather my tools.

"Who says I'm not?"

"The one who's about to plunge a needle into your skin."

Out of the corner of my eye, I see him smirk. "Maybe I've got a thing for pain."

I think of sinking my teeth into his lip when I kissed him. Now my face is definitely getting red. I do not need this distraction. Before my thoughts can betray me any further, I make sure my hands are steady and slide the needle into the skin at the edge of his detached thigh. I check his reaction, unsure how much he can feel in his unattached body parts. There's not so much as a flinch. Then I slide the needle through the skin under his knee, and he lets out the slightest hiss between his teeth.

"Still sticking with the 'I'm enjoying this' story?" I ask, though I don't take my eyes off the needle as my hands move through their work.

"Well, the view's certainly better than normal," he grits out.

I work carefully, occasionally glancing up at his expression, but he barely flinches, and his eyes stay locked on me. Despite everything, I am as gentle as I can be.

I place the needle and thread back into the case and take the scissors instead. Moving with deliberate slowness and care, I cut off the extra thread from his stitching. "How does that feel?" I ask.

He bends his knee and straightens it again, his eyes moving to look down at his body instead of me for the first time. "Feels—"

I lunge to my feet. When he glances up again, I'm holding both the scissors and the scalpel to his neck. I place the blades where the line of stitches crosses under his jawline. If he has a weak point, I suspect it will be there. Decapitating him may not kill him, but it should at least incapacitate him for a while.

"I don't want to hurt you," I whisper. "But I will if you try to stop me from walking out the door right now. Get up and move out of the way."

Victor's face slowly splits into a grin. He leans his head back so that his throat is only further exposed to me, and makes no sign of moving like I ordered him to. "Go ahead," he says, a sort of dark glee in his voice. "Do it. I dare you."

He's bluffing. He must be. I determined in our sessions together that he has a strong pain tolerance, but he *does* feel, and this will *have* to hurt. It'll slow him down. I've bided my time and waited for this moment. This is my chance—maybe my *one* chance—to get away. To save us both from this insane revenge plot. But as I will myself to cut into his flesh, my hand trembles.

He grabs my wrist. Instead of pushing me aside, as I know he could, he yanks me closer so I'm practically sitting on his lap. The edge of the scalpel cuts into his skin, neatly parting the skin but drawing no blood. "I said do it," he snarls, without so much as a flinch.

Do it, Lucy, I tell myself. *Do it and go free. He's bluffing!*

But I think of him shutting his eyes in pain. His face when he told me that no one had ever asked him about painkillers before. His voice when he said *I didn't expect you to be kind.* I freeze, staring down at him, and then whisper a curse and let go of my weapons.

Victor grins as they clatter to the floor. His cold fingers still hold my wrist in a viselike grip. "I knew it," he whispers. Then he leans over and presses his lips to mine.

Chapter Twenty-Four

I wish I could say that I recoil or make a calculated decision. But the truth is that there's not a coherent thought in my head as I meet his kiss, just pure, unadulterated *want*. My lips part and he groans into my mouth. He releases my wrist and grips the back of my neck instead, firm but not painful, as his cold tongue slides against mine. It sends a shiver down my spine, but not in a bad way. His touch is pleasantly cool against my hot skin, and he can't seem to get enough of my warmth. His hand pulls me flush against his chest. My legs fall on either side of his thighs, straddling him on top of the armchair.

This kiss is different than the one in the diner. There's no audience to perform for, no pretense that we're doing this for any reason other than wanting to, despite the fact I was holding a blade to his neck just seconds ago. I grab the front of his shirt, devouring his kisses with every bit of enthusiasm he's giving me. I'm barely aware of the lingering sting of my cuts from the diner.

There are so many reasons we shouldn't be doing this. He was—is?—my patient. I am—was?—here against my volition. But it's hard to think about this when our mouths meet again and again and again, both of us rough and needy.

My breath hitches at the chill of his hand slipping under the bathrobe and across my stomach. It feels so different, so *good*, a cool balm for the heat rising under my skin. I rock my hips against him, grinding down on the hard length I feel pressing against the confines of his briefs. He can get so hard even though he has no blood flow. How *curious*. I want to ask questions, but now isn't the time.

"Yeah, I never bought that good-girl act," he says. He sucks my earlobe between his teeth and tweaks my nipple between two fingers, hard enough to make me gasp and moan. "You're a nasty little thing, aren't you?"

Heat rushes to my face. I'm not usually like this, but he brings out something new in me, and it's embarrassing to have it called out. Yet it somehow only intensifies the ache between my legs, making me grind against his lap with more urgency. He grabs me and maneuvers me so I'm straddling one of his thighs instead, and I gasp at the friction between my legs.

"That's right," he murmurs, his hand on my lower back, urging the motion against him. "Show me how bad you want it."

I ride his thigh with only my panties separating skin from skin, the sensation dragging little moans out of me. It's unreal how good this feels, and it's even hotter with Victor's hand on me and his eyes locked on my face. But just as that liquid heat starts to build in me, embarrassment strikes. Am I really going to come like this, grinding against his thigh with both of us still partially clothed, like some horny virginal teenager? I've always struggled to let go during hookups, and self-consciousness holds me back now. I lean forward and bury my face in his shoulder to muffle the sounds I'm making and conceal my expression. But even as I try to stop, Victor's hand keeps moving me against him, controlling my body with all the ease of moving a doll.

"Don't stop," he whispers. "You're so fucking hot right now, Lucy. Come for me."

"I-I can't—" I break off and bite my lip.

"Yes, you can. I feel how wet you are. You're gonna come just like this, and then I'm gonna toss you on that bed and fuck you."

His certainty, the arrogance of it, should make me furious. But instead, it only turns me on more. My breath comes in short bursts, and I press my face into the crook of his neck as he keeps moving me against him. Heat builds between my thighs. My legs shake, and before I know it, I'm doing exactly what he told me to do, crying out and bearing down on his thigh as pleasure rolls through my entire body. He holds me while I gasp and tremble through the orgasm.

It leaves me feeling weak...and far from satisfied. Like it only stoked the flames higher. When Victor reaches down to push my panties to the side and runs a finger over my arousal, I sink my teeth into his shoulder, muffling a groan against his skin, and he shudders beneath me.

"Fuck," he mutters, and stands. He grabs me by the waist and lifts me effortlessly, heedless of the fact he still has only one hand. He carries me to the bed and pushes me onto it, face-down and ass up, before climbing on it behind me. He yanks the bathrobe up around my hips, then grabs the back of my head and pushes me further down into the mattress. I whimper, turned on by the way he takes charge like this—but before I can lose myself to poor judgment, I say, "Wait."

He instantly releases his grip on my head. "Too rough?"

"No," I say. "It's just, do we need a condom?" As impatient

as I am for this, I don't get laid nearly often enough to be on birth control, and I am *not* interested in becoming a mother. Even though part of me is curious about what a half-undead baby could look like. It'd be an interesting experiment if—no. No, no. This is not the time for that.

"I can't get you pregnant, if that's what you're asking," he says.

That piques my curiosity. "How interesting. But you still get erections. And orgasms, presumably, since you're—"

His hand grips the back of my head again and tugs at my hair.

"With all due respect, Doc," he says, his voice low and rough, "I haven't gotten laid in years, and you've been teasing me all day. Can I fuck you now or what?"

As I feel the head of his cock rub over my ass, I moan into the mattress.

He tugs harder at my hair, wrapping it around his fist. "Answer me."

"Yes," I gasp out. "Please. Fuck me."

He chuckles, releases me, and I hear him spit in his palm. I twist in his grip so I can look back at him, and a zip of nerves runs through me as I see him running his hand along a *very* impressive, very hard pierced cock. But a moment later, as if sensing my hesitation, he moves his hand between my legs instead of pushing into me. He runs a finger over the slick heat at the apex of my thighs and bites back a groan.

"So wet for me," he murmurs, and presses a thick finger inside me. It's been ages since anything's been inside me, but I'm so turned on that it slides in easily. My back arches, and this time the groan rips free from his mouth. "And so warm. Jesus." He adds a second finger to curl inside of me, and I whimper as he finds that sweet spot. I try to grind back against him, but he pushes me down with his handless arm. "Don't be greedy," he says, slowly fucking me with his fingers. I moan and squirm under his touch, aching for more. It's been so long since anyone touched me like this, longer yet since it was someone I actually care about. It terrifies me to admit that about Victor, but I can't deny it anymore.

He brings me to the edge of an orgasm, but just as my thighs start to tremble, he pulls his fingers free. Before I can voice a complaint, the sensation is replaced by the pressure of his cock against my entrance.

Even as wet as I am, I feel the stretch and a flicker of pain as he pushes into me. Still, I roll my hips against him, and he echoes my moan as I take more of him in. The strange coldness of him inside of me is indescribable, and I want—*need*—more of it.

"God," he mutters, his fingers digging into my hip. "You're so tight. You feel so fucking good." Yet still he pushes into me so agonizingly slowly. My fingers fist in the blankets, and I rock my hips back against him, greedy for more. "*Fuck*," he hisses. "Lucy. I told you it's been a while. Stop that or this'll be over too fast."

I might be more inclined to agree if he didn't just deny me a desperately needed orgasm. And yes, there is a sort of wicked glee in the idea of getting him to cum so fast. So I pretend to comply until he relaxes his grip on me, and then push my hips back against him hard and fast, so that he sinks fully into me.

There is no word for the sound he makes—a tortured, stran-gled half-moan, half-sigh. His fingers dig into my hips hard enough to bruise as he holds me still, and I can sense him grappling for control, trying not to tumble over the edge then and there.

"You," he says, "are a very bad girl."

"What are you going to do about it?" I whisper. I try to thrust back on him again, but he presses me down prone on the bed and settles enough of his weight on top of me that it's impossible for me to move. His muscular chest presses against my back and his arm wraps around my waist, holding me still.

"You don't get to be in control of this, Lucy," he murmurs in my ear. He slowly sinks into me, and I moan. "You're gonna take exactly what I give you. Nothing more and nothing less."

He fucks me slow and deep, pressing me down into the mattress with each thrust. I whimper at the way he stretches me, but like he said, I'm helpless to do anything but accept what he wants to give me. Ever so slowly, the coil of pleasure inside winds tighter.

Luckily for me, his control doesn't last long. Soon his hips start to slap against mine harder, faster, and he whispers a curse. The cheap motel bed squeaks as he slams into me again and again, making me cry out, the sound muffled by the bedsheets. I'm close, so close—

"Shit," he says, guttural and breathy. "I can't— *Lucy*—"

With that final moan, his movements go rough and choppy as he spills himself inside me.

I'm still throbbing as he pulls out, not quite at my own peak, but I try not to be disappointed. It's not as though it hasn't happened before. And he already got me off once, so...

Then I squeak in surprise as his strong, cold hand grabs me by the hips and flips me over onto my back. Before I can voice a question, he lowers himself to the bed between my legs and presses his mouth to me. I gasp, back arching, as his tongue slides against me. It's cold and wet as it flicks over my hot skin, a surprising enough sensation even before the zing of his piercing against my clit. I'm already aching and sensitive, messy with my own desire and his load. He laps and licks and sucks at me like he's desperate for the taste. His fingers dig into my skin, and his mouth is forceful enough to press me down into the mattress, so intense it's just on the verge of overwhelming but it's also exactly, *exactly* what I need—

And soon I'm spilling over the edge with a whimpering cry, one ankle wrapped over his back and my hands yanking at his hair to hold him where I need him as I quake and arch under his tongue. He moans against me and I grind against his mouth, my lips parted in a silent cry as pleasure shivers through me from head to toe. It feels like it goes on forever, and Victor lazily flicks his tongue all the way through, each flick of that piercing making me crest again. Finally, I go limp beneath him, releasing my grip on his hair with a shudder of pleasure.

He lifts himself up and rolls onto his back on the bed beside me, and I curl up against him.

"My bad," he mutters, without opening his eyes. "Like I said. Been a while."

"No complaints," I say, smiling even though he can't see it. I feel...lighter...after that, my whole body pleasantly sore, my limbs loose and relaxed. "And there's always next time."

His lips quirk even though his eyes stay shut. "Next time, huh?"

I'm grateful he's not looking as color floods my cheeks. *Right.* It takes a moment for reality to sink in about what just happened. I'm not ready to think about what this means, about how my plan for escape somehow turned into us fucking, so I try to hold it at bay by making a joke. "Well, of course. No good woman of science would perform an experiment only once..."

He huffs a breath. "You better not put any of this in your

little notebook about me."

I laugh, some of my tension easing. He still seems relaxed, so maybe reality can stay at arm's length for a little while longer. "I think it's safe to say this research has become personal in nature. But I may need to try a few more rounds before I come to any conclusions..." I pause and arch an eyebrow as I notice that he's already growing hard again. "Really? Is this science talk turning you on?" I wrap my fingers around his thick length, keeping a loose grip as I slowly slide my hand up and down, enjoying the feeling of him stiffening beneath my hand. "What a remarkable refractory period..."

"One of the perks of being undead, I guess." His breath hitches, undercutting the nonchalant tone.

"That and no risk of pregnancy?" I bite my lip, increasing the motion of my hand. "You're perfect."

He opens his eyes to look at me, and there's a spark of something I can't read in their mismatched depths. But when he starts to sit up, I press my free hand to his chest and urge him to lie back. "Relax," I whisper. "I want to take care of you."

Something odd, almost soft, crosses his face. Then he shuts his eyes again and lies back, though he turns his head to the side so I can barely see his face. "Harder," he murmurs.

I'm sore from how hard he fucked me, but I still feel a pulse of desire at being told what to do like that. I bite my lip and do as he says, increasing the pressure until he grunts and says, "Yes, like that."

I'm holding him so tightly that I'd be afraid of hurting a normal man, but I suppose I shouldn't be making assumptions when it comes to Victor. I think back to how he reacted when I bit his shoulder, and a thought occurs to me. I dig the nails of my free hand into the flat plane of his stomach. "Do you like pain?"

He groans, the muscles of his torso tightening. "Fuck. Yes, Lucy. More."

I scrape my fingernails across his shaft as I jerk him off, and he rewards me with a moan, his hips lifting up off the bed to chase the sensation. I grow bolder, gripping him harder and faster, dragging my nails hard against his skin. Every time I fear I might go too far, it only seems to drive him wilder, until he's moaning with abandon and thrusting up into my hand, and I know he's close.

I watch in fascination as his balls draw up and his legs shake. His cock pulses in my hand as he groans his way through an orgasm, sending thick spurts of cum up over his stomach.

"Fascinating," I murmur, still stroking one finger lazily over his dick, thinking idly about how his body works.

He looks over at me and grins. "You just did that because you had to see it yourself, didn't you?"

I flush at being caught but can't help but grin back at him. "That was one of my reasons." I tighten my grip on his shaft again, squeezing hard enough to hurt, and am rewarded by the way he stiffens in my hand once more. "But don't worry, Victor." I lick my lips. "There are plenty more experiments to run."

Chapter Twenty-Five

In the middle of the night, I wake in a viselike grip. Victor has his arms wrapped around my waist and his face buried in my hair, his huge body curved around mine. My lips quirk upward despite myself. I never would've imagined him to be the cuddly type. Nor would I think it could be so pleasant to be snuggled up against, well, a walking corpse. I've always preferred sleeping alone; I run hot, and sharing a bed in the past usually meant I'd wake up sweaty and cranky about having my space being crowded. But Victor's skin is pleasantly cool against me, a perfect contrast to the warmth of the covers.

He's also out cold, as far as I can tell. It'd be a good chance to slip out the door and away...if not for his tight hold on me. There's no way I can get away without waking him up.

It's a perfect excuse to stay here. To cuddle up closer to his chest and let myself fall back asleep. This changes nothing. I'll escape tomorrow, I tell myself. Tomorrow.

Just as I'm drifting off, I swear I feel him shift and pull me closer, almost as if he isn't asleep at all.

* * *

I sit up slowly and slide my glasses on to look around the room. Victor isn't here—not in the rumpled bedsheets beside me, nor in his usual post guarding the door. The bathroom door is open and its space unoccupied too. I don't even see the hand lurking anywhere. Did he leave me here alone? It seems so.

But I'm not sure if I should take it as a sign of trust...or a sign that he's abandoned me completely. Maybe the guilt about holding me hostage became too much.

A lump rises in my throat at that thought for reasons I can't define. I should be grateful that he's gone, if that's truly the case. It means I'm safe. I'm free. I got what I wanted. Didn't I?

Before I can even begin to process that tangle of emotions, the door opens, and Victor steps inside. He stops when he sees I'm awake, shuts the door behind him, and lifts up a paper bag. "I got breakfast," he says.

My lips twitch upward despite my best efforts to suppress the smile. "What a sweet kidnapper you are."

He huffs a laugh. "Well, you *have* been an enormously accommodating captive."

It should probably be weird that we can joke about this situation, but it doesn't feel that way. Still, my smile fades as he settles on the edge of the bed with the bag between us. I'm not really sure how to act around him now. The lines between us were already blurred before, and now... Now I have no idea what to think.

But I can't resist the call of a fresh bagel. I grab it from the bag when he offers it. For a few minutes, while I stuff my face with sweet, sweet carbs and he chomps on a mouthful of bacon, things feel as normal as they've ever been between us.

Then we both finish, and awkwardness thickens the air.

He clears his throat. "How's your arm?"

I lift the arm of my robe to check the bandages. Thankfully, our activities last night didn't dislodge them. "It's fine."

Silence falls again.

"Lucy," he says. He runs his fingers through his hair, sighs. "I never should've dragged you this far. I'm going to let you go now."

I stiffen. I wasn't sure what he was going to say, but I certainly wasn't expecting that. "Oh, *now* you want to get rid of me?"

He gives me a wry look. "You're upset I'm no longer holding you captive?"

I huff. "Oh, please. We both know we're well beyond that narrative. I could've easily left while you were gone." If I'm being honest with myself, I never put my full determination into trying to escape.

"This is my battle to fight," he says. "I'm not going to put you at risk for it."

I eye him. "That thing that attacked at the diner. It was...like you."

Victor's jaw clenches. He looks down at his lap. "I was afraid she would try again. Use what she learned from me."

I shiver, thinking about its terrifying bulk, so different from Victor's uncanny beauty. "So your creator sent it after you. She knows you're coming."

"Guess so," he mutters. "Probably the MRF warned her."

"That means she's going to be ready to face you," I say. "With more of those things. She could have an *army* of those things—"

"She won't," he says.

"What makes you so sure?"

"She'd have trouble controlling an army. One is hard

enough." His jaw works, and he shakes his head slightly as if trying to dislodge a thought, or a memory. "That's what it's all about for her. Control."

My heart aches for him—and I don't have a counterargument for that. Especially because there's a part of me that understands that need, that *compulsion* to be in control, and I fear he sees that in me as well. But we're getting off topic. "You can't face this alone," I tell him.

"Watch me."

"You're falling apart," I tell him. "You might need me. Especially afterward."

There's a flicker of surprise in his eyes, and a suspicion I've held for a while becomes firmer in my mind.

"You don't think there's going to be an afterward." He turns away, refusing to meet my eyes. "Victor. It's not worth it. Why can't you just let it be? Why can't you let yourself be happy?"

"Because she'll get to be happy too!" he snaps, turning back to me with fire in his eyes. "It's not fair! It's not fucking fair! She can't get to be happy after what she did to me. I'd rather drag us both down to the depths of fucking hell."

I draw back, startled at the vehemence in his tone and the look in his eyes. There's that anger again. It breaks my heart that he feels that way, but it scares me too. If he's willing to sacrifice anything it takes to get his revenge—including his life, his happiness—how can I trust him not to sacrifice me as well? I think back to the diner incident, and a lump forms in my throat.

I've been a pawn to him this whole time. He already tricked me into letting my guard down once. Am I going to let myself fall for it again?

I'm only making a fool of myself, letting myself believe for a single second that this means something. That there could be a happy ending for people like us. That we would deserve it even if it's possible. We're just a pair of screw-ups; of course all we know how to do is hurt one another.

"We never should've done this," I whisper. I was foolish to ever think I could change anything for him.

There's a flicker of hurt across his face that almost makes me regret the words. But then his expression shutters and his eyes go cold. "You're right. It was a mistake."

Ice splinters in my chest at the same time heat rises to my face. Hurt, embarrassment, regret, a flood of emotions rushes through me. How could I have been this stupid? I always knew that getting close to people only ends in one way. How could I let myself feel something for someone who lied to and kidnapped me, of all people?

"Like I said," Victor says, "I'll let you go now." He won't meet my eyes. His posture is closed off, arms folded over his chest and jaw set. "You don't need to be involved anymore."

I take a deep breath, and another, trying to work up the willpower to just get up and walk away, exactly like he wants me to. I should leave him to his own path of self-destruction.

But my gut tells me if I walk out that door, I'll never see him again. And I can't seem to convince myself that would be a good thing, even with the way my chest aches right now.

"You're still falling apart," I whisper, finally raising my eyes to look at him, even though he won't meet my gaze. "You still need me."

"I'll be fine," he says.

"You won't." He knows that, too, even if he won't admit it. "If you're going through with this idiocy, you need to be at your full strength. Let me fix you up, at least. The stitches I made will hold better than the old ones."

He finally drags his gaze over to mine, his eyes narrowing in suspicion. "Why would you do that?"

"Why do you think, Victor?" I glower right back at him. "I care about you, despite my best efforts not to. Someone has to." Since he clearly couldn't give a damn about his own life. I shake my head, trying not to get off track and throw us into another argument. Our time is limited, and I want to spend it wisely. "But I have one condition."

There's an immediate flash of stubbornness in his eyes. "I'm not going to stop going after her."

"That's not the condition." Only because I knew he'd never agree. He's obviously dead set on this, no matter the cost. And as much as it pains me to go along with it, I know he's too stubborn to let me talk him out of it. But maybe I can do something else to change his mind: *show* him the life he's missing out on. "I want you to take me out tonight. Give me one normal night with you."

His eyebrows lift. The look he gives me is full of clear suspicion. "Seriously?"

"Yes." I meet his gaze, all too serious about this. "You. Me. A date. That's the condition. I deserve at least one normal night with you before—" I hesitate, unsure how to end that sentence. The silence hangs in the air between us. "Before you risk everything for your revenge," I settle on, finally.

He eyes me. "If that's what you really want," he says, like he suspects I must have some secret plan. It hurts that he believes I must have an ulterior motive to want to spend time with him...though he's not entirely wrong. He isn't hearing what I have to say, so I hope tonight I can *show* him that he can still have a life. *A life with me*, I think, but I try to push the thought aside.

"I'm afraid you might be disappointed by the local options, though," he says. "This place isn't exactly known for its fine cuisine. Or...*any* kind of cuisine." His brow furrows. "Not that I'd be allowed in any place, looking like..." He gestures down at himself.

"I had something else in mind." I smile. "And haven't you looked at a calendar recently?" When he only gives me a blank look, I laugh. "If I've been keeping track of time accurately, I believe it's Halloween weekend, Victor. You don't need to hide tonight." I tilt my head, considering. "And as for where to go, well... Can you still drink alcohol?"

Chapter Twenty-Six

n hour later, we're walking into a bar. Victor has an arm slung around my shoulder, so I can feel the tension leak out of his body as he looks around and realizes no one is giving him a second glance. The bar is full of patrons wearing ridiculous costumes and doused in fake blood. It's the only time of the year that his stitches and green-tinged skin will blend in with the crowd. His "costume" consists of a pair of ripped jeans and a shirt left mostly unbuttoned.

As for me, after a stop at a local party shop, I whipped together a quick outfit involving a lab coat and a pair of goggles pushed up on my forehead, worn over a simple crop top and tight pencil skirt. A mad scientist of sorts. I wasn't sure if it was in poor taste, given Victor's background, but when he saw me step out of the dressing room, he just about keeled over with laughter. I've never seen him so amused before; it warmed my heart, hearing that genuine throaty laugh come out of him.

"Sick costume, bro," an inebriated man slurs as he walks past, punching Victor in the shoulder.

We exchange a look and laugh, the second time he's laughed tonight. It feels like a victory already.

"See? What'd I tell you?" I ask, squeezing his arm.

In the dim lighting and the Halloween crowd, with that uncharacteristically cheerful look on his face, he really does look like an entirely different person. A living, breathing person. It makes my heart ache, to imagine who he was before all of this happened to him.

He may not know it, but he's not the only one pretending to be a normal person tonight. This isn't the sort of thing I do. I'm not much of a drinker, nor really much of a social person at all. I can count the number of times I've been to a bar on one hand, and I've never been out on a night as busy as tonight. But I wasn't going to pass up on Victor's one chance all year to walk around in the world without fear of sticking out in the crowd. And it's worth it to see his tense shoulders relax and a small lopsided smile bloom on his face.

I'm afraid I don't quite know what to do now that we're here, but Victor guides me over to the bar with a hand on my lower back. He glowers at someone about to snag the last open stool until the man backs off. Then he graciously pulls it out for me and stands at my side.

When I watch him lean on the bar to order a shot and then he swallows his whiskey without so much as a grimace, I feel like I'm getting a glimpse of what he was like when he was alive. It makes me wonder, uncomfortably, whether or not we would've gotten along when he was alive.

He seems so natural here. Unlike me. I'm tenser than I expected to be, with all of the noise and the crowd around us. I have the uncomfortable feeling of eyes on me, but when I look over my shoulder, it's hard to make out any faces in the blur of the dance floor.

Victor slams a shot on the bar in front of me, and I startle.

"Oh. Thank you." I shake off my sense of unease and pick it

up. I take it in three tiny sips, making a face the whole while, and am rewarded for my efforts by a sly smile from Victor as he orders another round right away.

"If I end up sloppy drunk, you have no one but yourself to blame," I tell him, before grimacing through another sipped shot. At least it will make me less nervous.

He throws his own back without a flinch, and then leans in, his lips close against my ear. His hand squeezes my knee. "Maybe I like you sloppy."

I blush and place a hand on his chest to playfully push him away. But he catches my wrist, a glimmer of mischief in his eye. I feel something move under my skirt.

"What the..." I squirm, stiffening up.

"Shh," Victor says, grinning. He pulls back and leans on the bar again, and I notice that the sleeve closest to me gapes open at the end. The hand that was just squeezing my knee is gone.

"You *brought* the *hand*?"

"I told you it's got a mind of its own," he says with a shrug. "Plus, I might've fantasized about this for a while."

"You can't just—" I cut off, biting my lip and squeezing my thighs as his hand crawls higher. "*Victor.*" I glance around, but of course, the patrons around us are all drunk and oblivious. My skirt is long enough to disguise what's happening, and my legs are tucked under the bar anyway.

Still, this feels so...*public.* Which should not send a shiver of excitement through me. I definitely should not be slowly sliding my thighs apart to allow him access. And yet...

"That's my girl," Victor murmurs, and slides another shooter across the bar to rest in front of me. "Relax. Have a drink."

I swallow hard and reach a trembling hand for the shot glass. I sip. It's something deceptively sweet, with only a bite of alcohol. The fingers beneath my skirt wander between my legs. Instead of merely pushing my panties to the side, the hand crawls inside of them and rests there, palming the heat where my thighs meet.

I bite back a whimper and force myself to gulp down the rest of my shot. Victor rests his elbows on the bar and chats with the bartender while his hand starts to stroke me under my skirt. I can't focus enough to hear the conversation or do anything other than sit and bite my lip and try not to cry out. By the time one cold finger slides inside of me, I'm so wet, there's barely any friction. A second one slips in beside it, and I gasp, grabbing the edge of the bar. Victor grins but doesn't look at me as his fingers curl inside of me and stroke that sweet spot, coaxing the fire inside of me to burn hotter and hotter until—

A whimper slips out despite my best efforts, and I white-knuckle the edge of the bar to keep my body from spasming as pleasure crashes over me. My toes curl and my thighs tremble. Victor glances sideways at me and holds eye contact as I clench hard around his fingers. His hand continues its deliciously slow movement until I sag against the stool.

Then Victor leans down to kiss me and surreptitiously grabs his hand from under my skirt until he straightens again.

"You're wicked," I murmur.

"Guilty as charged," he says, and raises his hand to his lips, surreptitiously flicking his tongue against the fingers that were inside of me. I blush furiously, and his smirk widens.

"Dance with me," he says, and I let him pull me to my feet and into the crowd.

It's sweaty and cramped and loud, and I can feel myself stiffening despite my intention to be normal tonight. But when Victor pulls me flush against him and brackets his arms around me to keep the crowd at bay, I relax against him.

He holds me as I sway to the music, one arm around my waist, his chest against my back. I'm a terrible dancer, always too stiff and awkward and too hyperaware of my body to move smoothly, but it doesn't matter when I'm lost in the crowd and I have Victor with me.

As the shots I took settle into a light buzz—yes, I'm aware I'm a lightweight—and the recent orgasm relaxes me, my body begins to loosen up. The music is so loud that I can feel the thrum of the beat vibrating through me. I move along with it, getting more daring, pressing my ass back against Victor and imitating the grinding motion I've always been too nervous to pull off before.

Judging by the way his hand tightens on my hip—and something firm pokes against me from behind—I suspect that I'm doing a decent job. After a few minutes of teasing him, I turn around and wrap my arms around his neck, smiling up at him before I lean in to whisper, "You remember when we were in that gas station bathroom?"

He huffs a laugh, his hand on my waist sliding down to cup my ass. "I remember," he says, his voice low and his eyes locked on mine.

"Mm." I bite my lip. "What do you say to a redo?"

Without a word, he spins me around and marches me to the bathroom, elbowing his way through the crowd without a single glance at the people who shoot him dirty looks. I laugh, murmuring apologies as we go.

He drags me straight past the line for the women's room and into a stall. It smells like sweat and weed in here, and people snicker as they see us, but I can't bring myself to care. I've never done anything like this in my life. I've always tried so hard to be good, to be responsible. But Victor brings out a side of me that I didn't know existed.

He pushes me against the stall wall from behind and kicks my feet apart with one boot. I arch my back and let him yank my panties down to my ankles. But when I hear him undoing his belt, I whirl around to face him instead, grabbing him by the front of the shirt.

"Why are you always trying to fuck me from behind?" I ask. It's hot, but still... "I wanna see your face."

Something unexpected flickers across his expression. "This face?" His smile is lopsided, a little bitter. "You don't have to pretend, Lucy."

"Victor." I reach up to cup his face, slide my thumb over the torn section of his cheek. "I'm not pretending. I love your face." I lean in and kiss the scarred edges, then move lower and kiss the line of stitches on his throat. "I love every stitch. Every scar. Because they're part of you. They're part of what make you the man I know."

I wouldn't be talking like this, throwing around the word *love*, if I weren't tipsy. But right now I feel loose, free, a little wild. I lick the side of his neck where his pulse should beat, and feel his throat move under my mouth as he swallows.

"Lucy," he says hoarsely.

I nip at his jaw, move my hand down to the front of his pants to unzip him, and slide a hand into his boxers.

"I mean it," I whisper. "I think you're perfect. Perfectly flawed. I've wanted you since I first saw you." I work him slowly with my hand, squeeze him as he hardens, and lean back just enough that I can look up and meet his eyes. "So let me see you."

He stares at me then mutters a curse, pushes my hand away,

and grabs me by the hips to lift me up. I wrap my legs around him as he shoves me back against the wall.

He pushes into me hard enough that I cry out, loud enough that I know the other people in this bathroom can hear me over the pounding music. I don't care. I'm out of my own head, for once; I can't bring myself to think about anything but him right now. Victor, letting me look him in the face as he fucks me against the bathroom stall. I grab a fistful of his hair and yank his head back so I can see his eyes. He looks as wild and hungry as I feel.

His hips pump fast and hard, and I pull his hair and claw his back and moan his name until I'm no longer capable of forming coherent sounds, just wordless cries as he thrusts into me. There's a dangerous sort of intimacy to this, an intensity in his eyes that would frighten me if I didn't trust him so much.

"Oh, fuck," he says. "*Lucy.*" He bites my shoulder as he comes, and the unexpected spark of pain drags me down over the edge with him.

"Yes, yes, *yes,*" I chant, my legs holding him against me, my head thrown back, his teeth in my skin and his cock pulsing inside of me as we finish together.

* * *

We stumble through the motel door, smelling of the club—all sweat and smoke and alcohol, with a hint of rough sex in the bathroom. I insist on dragging him into the shower before bed. He tolerates my drunken antics, bending over so I can shampoo his hair for him, rolling his eyes when I ask too many questions about whether or not he needs to clean his stitches. And when the long night finally catches up with me and I can barely keep my eyes open, he towels me off, helps me into the hotel robe, and carries me to bed. I make myself comfortable in the grip of his big arms, burrowing my face against his bare chest.

I lie there, breathing in his leathery scent and slowly sobering up. I think about how many opportunities I had tonight to get away. To call the MRF and have Victor put back in his cell. He'd be safe. And he'd hate me.

But that isn't what stopped me. Every time the thought crossed my mind, it felt wrong. Because...as much as I hate what he might choose, I still can't bring myself to deny him the choice. He doesn't deserve that, especially after everything he's been through. He should choose his own path.

Still, as I press myself against him and swallow back the urge to cry, I wish, desperately, that he would choose me.

Just when I'm about to doze off, he whispers, "I'm not going back to that place."

I jerk awake, blinking up at him in the darkness. "I would never ask that of you."

He runs one finger down over my chest and stomach. "I don't know where else to go," he says. "If we were to...to run." He pauses, exhales. "Revenge is the only future I've ever imagined for myself. I don't know what else to do."

That's enough to fight through the lingering hazes of both sleep and alcohol in my mind. He's tiptoeing around the subject, but I still get the gist of what he's saying. He's thinking of options other than going after his creator. "We could find someplace to disappear," I say. "We'll figure it out. I promise, Victor. There are options."

He pulls me closer and rests his chin on the top of my head. "Okay," he murmurs.

"We can talk about it in the morning," I say, and yawn.

"Yeah." He strokes a hand over my hair. "Okay. Sleep, Lucy."

So I do.

Chapter Twenty-Seven

I wake to the sound of shattering glass.

I jolt upright in bed, disoriented and barely able to see in the dark room. Victor reacts faster than me, rising from bed and lunging toward the figure climbing through our broken window.

"What the f—" I exclaim, barely able to see what's happening aside from two silhouettes grappling in the darkness.

"Lucy!" Victor shouts. "Get back!"

I grab my glasses, half tumble out of bed, and crawl across the floor to my medical bag. I can barely see what I'm doing, but my fingers are well-accustomed to the weight of a scalpel in my hand. I grab it and rise to my feet, whirling back to where Victor is fighting off the unknown assailant.

It's that creature from the diner. I can tell by its hulking form, dwarfing even Victor's height. But what truly scares me is the silence. Victor emits small sounds as he struggles—grunts of effort, a low sound of pain that wrenches my heart—but the stranger makes no sound at all as it wraps a hand around Victor's upper arm. At first, I wonder why it isn't going for a more vital target—but then it wrenches hard to the side, and stitches pop. It yanks Victor's arm off his body.

I scream. So does Victor, an awful raw cry torn from deep in his throat. I've never heard him make a sound like that, not even with a needle sliding into his skin. I lunge forward without even thinking about it, scalpel raised above my head, and thrust it straight into the side of the creature's neck.

Even with my scalpel sinking in to the hilt, it doesn't so much as flinch, nor utter a sound. It lifts Victor off his feet and tosses him out through the open window. Only then does the beast reach up, yank the scalpel out of his neck, and let it clatter to the floor.

"Victor!" I shriek, the reaction delayed by my utter horror at what just happened. I stumble forward, intending to rush to see if he's still okay—God, let him be okay—but then the creature turns to look at me, and I stop.

My eyes are finally adjusting to the dark room, and I catch glimpses of the face of our enemy. The harsh features segmented by lines of stitching. The fact that one arm is longer than the other, giving him an awkward lopsided slouch. The tint of gray to his skin. It is mismatched in the same way that Victor is, but with none of Victor's fascinating beauty. This is a monster shaped with utter cruelty in mind, and when my eyes meet its, there is no intelligence or warmth in their dark depths. I can't even think of it as a *him*; there is nothing alive in its slack, gruesome features.

I know that this creature was created by the same hands as Victor. But if Webster made Victor with the goal of creating life, she made this thing with the goal of creating a *weapon*. It looks like it could snap me in half with a single hand, without a shred of remorse. I take a step back despite myself. I should run, grab something to defend myself, barricade myself in the bathroom...but I don't think any of it would even slow this monster down. And I'm so scared, I can't seem to move, can barely even breathe as I stare up at it.

But it's not here for me. And after a moment, it turns and lumbers for the window, still gripping Victor's arm. It climbs through the broken glass with no heed for the jagged edges biting into its skin.

"Victor," I whisper. My feet won't move. "Victor," I say again, almost a sob this time, and finally I manage to stumble to the door. "Victor, *run!*"

The monster jumps off the motel balcony and lands in the parking lot with an earth-shaking impact. I race out after it and grab on to the railing, staring down.

In the parking lot, Victor is managing to struggle to his feet after being thrown. His left arm is missing from the shoulder down, and one of his legs is twisted at a terrible angle. He manages to climb to his feet and turn to face the creature with gritted teeth and fire in his eyes.

The lumbering giant advances on him, and he lunges toward it with a cry.

"No," I shout, and run for the stairs. I can't see what's happening, but I can hear a terrible ripping sound, and a gurgled cry from Victor. By the time I make it down to the parking lot, it's already done. I stumble to a stop and press a hand to my mouth in horror as I see the creature standing. One of its massive hands is holding Victor's body up by the waist...and the other is clutching his severed head.

I don't think about my own safety or my impossible odds. I fling myself at the creature with a cry of blind fury, reaching for Victor's head. The beast barely acknowledges me; it simply turns and elbows me away. The movement is so easy, so casual, but it hits me with enough force to throw me to the asphalt.

CHAPTER TWENTY-SEVEN

The pain is intense; I barely keep the contents of my churning stomach down.

By the time I manage to blink away the tears and struggle to my feet, the creature is already tossing Victor's body into the back of a truck and climbing into the driver's seat. I run toward it again, asphalt tearing up my bare feet, too panicked to even think about what I'm trying to do, but before I can reach it, the truck peels out of the parking lot. It turns onto the road and roars into the distance, taking Victor with it.

I slowly sink to my knees in the empty parking lot and let out a wail of despair.

Chapter Twenty-Eight

I'm not sure how much time passes. At some point, I limp back to the motel room. Part of me is surprised that nobody shows up to investigate the screams and the broken window, but another part recognizes that the place is practically abandoned. I suspect the only other person here is whoever is manning the front desk, and they certainly don't get paid enough to get involved in this shit.

I sit on the bed, feeling numb, until the sun rises. The light creeping through the broken window is enough to snap me out of my haze. I can't just wait here. I need to do something. I need to save Victor.

But as the thought rises, it sinks again in a rush of despair. I don't know if Victor is even alive. I know he can survive a lot, but that was a level of violence I've never seen before. And even if he's alive now, I have no doubt that thing is taking him back to their creator, who will know exactly how to destroy the life she made. Plus, even if I make it in time, who am I to stand against that *thing*? To outsmart a mad genius who brought the dead back to life?

Stupid. We were so stupid. All this time Victor was hunting his creator, we never took it seriously that we were being hunted too. Even after the warning shot at the diner, we only forged ahead. God only knows how long Webster has been tracking us. Maybe it was my insistence on going to that club that caught her attention, or maybe she's been waiting this whole time, and last night gave her the moment of vulnerability she needed.

But I force myself to push my regret aside. I don't have time for this wallowing. Victor needs me.

I force myself to stand up and walk over to his duffel bag, sorting through it until I find my car keys and my cell phone.

My cell phone is dead, but I could call the MRF from the motel's phone. They could provide backup for me. Send in some of those armed security officers of theirs, or Mara's favorite monster, to put down the monstrosity that ripped Victor apart and carried the pieces of him away from me. I'm sure I could convince them that it's a noble cause.

But if I did that, Victor would end up locked in a cell again too. I doubt the MRF will look kindly upon him using me as a hostage and kidnapping me, even if I try to argue in his favor. I don't know anyone working there well enough to trust them as an ally, and I don't have time to waste trying to convince them of the truth. Plus, I know Victor. He would never want me to save his life just to land him back in that place. I once convinced myself it would be worth it to save him, but now... I won't betray him like that.

But I won't abandon him either. My chances are slim if I go on my own, but I have to try. He needs me. He's been left behind far too many times; I won't let him face these demons alone.

I don't know where to find his creator's lab, but there must be some clues in the car. And I do know it can't be far. Victor himself said that she must've sent the creature after us because we were getting close.

So I change out of the hotel robe and into some of the clothes Victor bought for me, and head out to the car, duffel bag over one shoulder and surgery kit clutched in my hand. I set it all on the passenger seat and take the driver's spot. The car smells like crinkled leather and musk—smells like *Victor*—enough to make my chest ache, but I push it aside and rummage around for anything of use. I find a gun in the glove box, check to make sure that it's loaded, and put it back.

A tap against the window nearly makes me jump out of my skin.

But my scream catches in my throat and turns into a startled intake of breath as I see a hand clinging to the side of the car. *Victor's* hand. The creature that took Victor away didn't collect it with the rest of him. I slowly open the door and reach out to grab it; the hand grabs me back, cold fingers intertwining with mine. I swallow hard, pull it into my lap, and shut the door again.

"Victor," I whisper, looking down at the severed hand that's all I have left of him. I hold on tight and hope that, wherever he is, he can feel the warmth as I squeeze his fingers.

But this hand isn't just some emotional keepsake. It's something I can use to find Victor and help him. He said it has a mind of its own when it's detached from his body, right?

"Victor..." I say again. I feel foolish talking to a hand, but I push it aside. There's no room for the logic of the normal world right now. What I need is the logic of *Victor*, my beloved impossibility. "Do you know where the rest of your body is?" I carefully lift the hand up, set it on the dashboard, and hope.

The hand stands upright on its fingers. It turns from side to side, as if *looking*. Then it lifts one finger and points.

I let out a breath, following its finger toward the horizon as if I can see beyond it if I try hard enough. I don't know if I'm being led by Victor or just some scrap of consciousness left in his hand. I don't know what will be left of Victor when—if—I find him. But I do know that wherever he is, that thing that took him will be too. And so will his creator. The woman so horrible that Victor was willing to throw away anything and everything, including his own happiness and including me, to destroy her.

It will be dangerous. Wherever I'm going, there will be a fight to save Victor, and to survive at all. And I'm risking everything for a man who held me hostage, kidnapped me, and was willing to leave me behind to pursue his vengeance.

But he is also a man who has held me in his arms and kissed me, shown me kindness and care. Who is so broken, he doesn't think he deserves gentleness in return. Whatever I face, I know that we will face it together.

So when it comes down to it, the choice isn't hard at all.

"All right, then." I put the keys in the ignition and turn on the car. "Let's find the rest of you."

Chapter Twenty-Nine

A day passes, and then a night, and another. I stop only to shop for essentials and sleep on the side of the road. Then I shake myself awake and keep going. Sometimes I feel like I'm going insane, driving days through the endless desert, guided only by the severed hand sitting on my dashboard and a stubborn spark of hope in my heart.

The more time I spend looking for Victor, the more I fear what will be left when I finally find him. I can't bring myself to try to imagine what Webster could be doing to him. She's the one that created him; she'll know how to take him apart too. She could be torturing him, redoing all of those experiments I already read in far too much detail in his file. Or she could've killed him already. I'm not sure which one I should hope for.

But even if she isn't doing any of that... She won't be feeding him. Which means Victor is going to be hungry when I find him. *Very* hungry.

When I think back to our last encounter when he was in that state, I grip the steering wheel so tightly that my knuckles turn white. My breaths get shallow and panicky.

I can't deny it: I'm scared. I'm so goddamn scared. But I'm not going to let that prevent me from doing whatever I can to find him. No matter what's left, he is worth saving. I know that with every fiber of my being.

So I follow as Victor's hand leads me through the desert, off the major highways and into a maze of narrow, winding side roads—then on and on until it dwindles to a single narrow dirt path, into the mountains that were once on the distant horizon. For a few hours, I start to wonder if I've made a grave mistake, because there seems to be nothing here but cacti and an increasing amount of trees as we head up a mountain path.

But just when I'm beginning to really question if I've been led into a trap in the middle of nowhere, the hand scuttles across the dashboard and taps on my steering wheel. I stop, blink my bleary eyes, and look around. For a moment, I see nothing— only the darkening trees around us as the sun sinks beneath the horizon to close out another day. *A third day since Victor has last eaten, if he's still alive at all*, a voice whispers in the back of my mind, but I push it aside. Finding him comes first; the rest comes later.

Then a light flickers through the trees. I swallow and pull the car forward to get a better look, and slowly, I make out the shape of a house in the trees. A single structure out in the middle of nowhere. It's unassuming on the surface, just a rustic little wooden cabin, not the sort of place I'd imagine a power-hungry scientist capable of bringing the dead to life would live.

But then I realize how far from civilization we are, how hidden this place is without a single sign to lead the way. And I note, too, the fact that this building has no windows. A sense of foreboding shivers down my spine.

This is the place.

The hand jumps off the steering wheel and into my lap. I

stroke it idly as it huddles against me. I hope the fact that it's still moving means that Victor's still alive in there somewhere, but I don't know for sure. All of this time researching Victor, and I still feel like I understand so very little.

I open the car door and carefully put the hand on the ground. "I don't know how this is going to go," I say. I don't know how much it understands, but I have to try. "You don't have to be a part of it."

After a beat of hesitation, the hand scurries off into the forest. Whether it intends to find another way to Victor or to get far away from here, I'm not sure.

As for me, I've made my choice. I reach into the glove compartment, take out the gun, and get out of the car.

I circle the building three times before I'm forced to admit that my initial impression was right. There are no windows, no back doors. There is no way inside other than the front entrance.

Perhaps it's for the best. I'm not cut out for stealth missions. But I do have a gift for chemistry from my med school days, which means that it's easy for me to concoct one hell of a distraction.

Contrary to a certain popular work of fiction, gasoline and orange juice will not make napalm. Not that I blame the creator; it would be irresponsible to publish a recipe for something so destructive. But suffice to say, it's not impossible for curious minds like mine to research such a thing, nor is it difficult to get one's hands on the real ingredients for that recipe...even at a Walmart in the middle of nowhere on my way here.

As I haul the canister out of the trunk, I'm aware of what a dangerous weapon I have in my hands. But I also know that from what I've seen of the creature I'm up against, a gun will have no effect. Maybe it won't be a quick and easy solution, but if I burn that thing hot enough, I believe it will work.

* * *

I start by setting a small fire in the forest near the cabin. Not a big blaze, but enough that it is a potential threat to Webster's hideout. Then I climb into a nearby tree and wait, watching the flames spread.

My heart pounds as I hide, every muscle tense. I know there are so many ways this could go wrong. The small fire blanket wrapped around my shoulders feels like flimsy armor. But I have to do something, and I don't have time to concoct a brilliant plan.

Soon enough, the door opens and the creature lumbers out. It seems even more lopsided and misshapen than normal, its gait dragging and strange. I feel a surge of triumph that Victor must have put up one hell of a fight. *That's my Victor.* Now it's my turn to prove I can be just as fierce.

The creature douses the flames with a bucket of water, and then scrapes dirt over it with one foot, all while craning its thick approximation of a neck to look around for who set the blaze. I sit frozen, watching, and see the moment it notices my car half hidden in the trees. It lets out a low sound—half grunt, half growl—and lumbers that way.

Right under the tree branch I'm waiting on.

I dump the gas can of my napalm-like concoction on its head, and it reels back, sputtering. Its head tilts back and it fixes its mean, dead eyes on me as it grabs the trunk of the tree.

While I fumble in my bag for my can of hairspray and lighter, the thick tree groans and shudders beneath me. My heart jumps into my throat. I did *not* think this thing had any way of getting me down from here—I thought if anything, it would climb— but instead it's taking the brute-force method of knocking the whole tree down, and it seems strong enough to do it. The tree shakes violently as the creature's obscene muscles bulge and strain. I cling to the branch with my legs while holding on to my pack with my arms. I catch glimpses of the creature beneath the shaking limbs of the tree: its beady eyes, the veins in its neck standing out, its teeth bared.

I can barely hang on, let alone get the lighter to work. I flick it desperately with my thumb, trying to get a flame to catch. Once, twice—

The creature roars. The tree's trunk lets out a mighty, horrible crack. The lighter tumbles from my fingers. I gasp, reaching for it—and slip as the tree tilts dangerously to one side.

The ground rushes up to meet me.

I land in an awkward half-crouch. The hairspray rolls away into the pine needles and dirt. But my attention immediately shifts to the hulking beast now extracting itself from the shredded, bent tree trunk. I knew it was big before, but it seems gargantuan now as it approaches me. I scramble on my hands and knees, a jolt of pain going through the leg that took the bulk of my weight, and grab the hairspray.

But the lighter. *The lighter.* Where the hell is it?

The creature grabs one of my legs and yanks me back through the dirt. I scream, flipping over and spraying it in the eyes in desperation. It roars but doesn't release me, instead shaking me like a dog with a toy. My head spins and my leg throbs. I remember the creature ripping Victor's arm off, and I wonder if my leg is about to meet the same fate.

"Let me go!" I scream. The words echo in the forest, but as they die away, it only seems to make the silence louder. There's no one around to hear me. No one around to help.

No one who will help Victor if I don't.

With that panicked thought flitting through my mind, I flip over again and, by some miracle, spot the lighter within reach. I scramble forward, taking advantage of the creature still swiping at its eyes, and grab it.

This time it only takes one flick of my thumb to light the flame.

I turn, eyes locked on that tiny flame that I hope will be my salvation, and lift the can of hair spray behind it. I aim at the towering corpse, the stink of gasoline thick in my nose, and I press down on the nozzle.

The flame is brighter than expected, a roar of fire in the creature's direction. It catches my homemade napalm and spreads with dizzying speed to consume the creature. The monster releases my leg and staggers back, screeching a horrible sound that makes me want to clasp my hands over my ears. Instead, I crawl forward on my knees and keep up the stream of flames.

The creature stumbles into the broken tree trunk, one thick hand smearing the flaming gunk on its skin all over it. The fire spreads. The monster falls to its hands and knees, clawing at itself and digging deep gouges in its own undead flesh. Chunks of it fall off, and the flames spread to the undergrowth and pine needles around us. I choke on the stench of burning flesh.

The spray from my makeshift flamethrower fizzles out, and I'm left holding it down with numb fingers for a few seconds before I realize. I click off the lighter and stare at the destruction I've wrought. The creature is keening, still alive somehow, and the fire is spreading to the forest around us, toward the building where I suspect Victor is kept.

No. I scramble to my feet, only for my left leg to immediately give out and send me slamming down on one knee again. I let out a cry of pain and hear an answering roar behind me.

My scream seems to have roused the monster. Somehow—still flaming, still losing chunks of charred flesh—it rises to its feet faster than I can and staggers toward me, one aflame hand outstretched. I force myself up and lurch forward, biting hard on the inside of my cheek and fighting through the pain as I flee through the trees. The fire is still spreading, the air thick with smoke.

I made a mistake. Especially because that goddamned creature is still alive and chasing me, even as pieces of it fall to the forest floor. It's slow, but so am I. And it seems like nothing will stop it from getting its vengeance on me.

As I look back over my shoulder, terror splintering cold in my chest, for a moment I see Victor flickering in the creature's place—his teeth bared in a grimace, his stitches popping out, still staggering along toward his one goal even if it kills him.

I whip my head around and keep limping until I reach the building. Slamming into the front door, I fumble for the knob, but it's locked.

I was hoping the creator would leave the door open for her pet to return. But maybe she's watching all of this right now, locking me out in the hope that thing can still finish me off. When I turn around to view it again, I see that the creature has lost one leg and its face is half melted off. It probably can't see, and can barely walk, but still it comes seeking me in a blind, stupid fury.

I could hide, wait for its undead life to flicker out or its corpse to become immobile, but then I'll still be stuck outside this locked building.

I think fast. Remembering the way it reacted to my cry of pain, I fist my hands at my sides, screw my eyes shut, and scream.

The creature lets out a hoarse answering cry and barrels toward me. I stand my ground until the very last second. Then I dive out of the way—twisting my injured ankle again as I thump belly-first onto the ground—and the creature's momentum carries it straight through the spot I was and into the door. I hear the sound of splintering wood behind me.

I slowly push myself up on my hands and knees. I'm trembling as I struggle to my feet, but I force myself to keep limping forward, dragging my left leg as I stumble past the destroyed front door and into the building.

I don't expect to find a cozy little cabin. A crackling fireplace, a moose head on the wall, a cheery rustic design. The picturesque effect is somewhat ruined by the gigantic monster face down on the hardwood floor, its smoldering stumps of fingers still clawing at the floorboards although the rest of its body seems to have given up the fight.

I carefully step toward it, looking around the room. There's no sign of Webster, or of Victor, or of anything I expected to find here. It looks so...normal.

A gurgle draws my attention back to the creature. *Definitely not normal,* I remind myself. This thing came from this building.

"Mas...ter."

The hair on the back of my neck rises as the thing speaks from its raw, ruined throat. I didn't know it could do that, and it strikes me with a wave of unwanted sympathy. Again I'm reminded of Victor, stuck following endlessly after his creator even when given freedom. Like a dog chasing its owner after being left on the side of the road. "Mas...ter..." The creature gurgles again and raises one of its still-flaming hands toward the fireplace along one wall.

I step around its body, looking that way. There's nothing but the fireplace and a bearskin rug thrown in front of it. No reason the creature would be trying to crawl *toward* the fire after it has been destroyed by it, unless...

I crouch, wincing in pain, and pull back the rug to reveal a hidden hatch in the floorboards beneath. Yet my triumphant smile fades as I look up at the creature again.

It doesn't look dangerous anymore, lying there with the flames dying out and its blinded eyes searching for a creator that didn't come to help it.

"I'm sorry," I say. "You deserved better."

But there is nothing more I can do for it, and I have my own monster to save. I raise the gun and shoot it in the head—twice, for good measure. The weight of the gun is unfamiliar in my hands, but at this range, it doesn't matter. The creature's hands thump to the floor, and it lies face down, at peace.

I lower the gun with a sigh. The noise will have alerted Webster that I'm inside the building and coming for her, if she wasn't already aware. But stealth has never been a part of the plan...and part of me relishes the thought that she's waiting. I hope she's afraid. Afraid like she's made both of her creations be over the years.

Let her know that I'm coming for her. And more importantly, let Victor know that he's not alone. That I came for him.

I pull open the hatch, revealing a staircase spiraling into darkness below, and limp my way toward the unknown.

Chapter Thirty

Now this looks like a mad scientist's lair.

The upstairs was a front. The basement is where the truth is laid bare. I step off the stairs into a room of cold metal and concrete lit by fluorescent bulbs above. The walls are lined with shelves, the shelves stacked haphazardly with...

With so many things. Things I wish I had the willpower to turn away from, but part of me is undeniably curious, and so instead I step forward to get a closer look. There are jars of liquid with a variety of forms suspended within: eyeballs and human fingers and tongues. Then there are the bones, stacked in neat piles by type: *tibia, fibula, ulna,* my brain provides helpfully before I force my eyes to move on. Because this isn't some medical school test. This is...sick. It makes me queasy to look at it, though I can't tear my eyes away.

Maybe this is the feeling that some people get when they look at my taxidermy and graphic medical textbooks. But the feeling here is so very different to me. I am fascinated by the human body because I want to understand it in order to *help*, and my taxidermy projects are an act of love. I find none of that here. This is the work of a person who enjoys taking things apart just for the sake of it.

That sense of wrongness only grows when I focus on the metal bed in the center of the room. The leather straps for restraints are reminiscent of the ones used on Victor at the MRF, but the tray of tools beside it—scalpels and scissors and forceps, along with a particularly nasty-looking bone saw— speak to more sinister intentions. So does the drain set in the floor beneath it, the metal and concrete around it stained a dark, rusty brown. The counter beyond the table holds a tripod for a camera, and stacks of folders and notebooks; one has been left open, revealing a hurried, messy scrawl, as if someone left in the middle of writing.

I hate this place instinctively. I have to keep fighting the urge to hold my breath, as if I'm breathing in tainted air. Awful things have happened here. Cruel things. Evil things.

A distant banging draws my attention to the door on the other side of the room. Foreboding makes my hair stand on end. I'm not alone down here, I know it... Webster is surely lurking, but Victor needs me, and from the way the smell of smoke is growing, the fire is still spreading above me. I have to free him before it overtakes the cabin. I limp toward the door and turn the knob. It opens with a creak, revealing a dark hallway. The banging is coming from the other end.

I head toward it, step by careful step, my eyes adjusting to the darkness. I pass a barred door revealing a small, empty concrete room within. Another door, this one solid metal, with no clues about what's on the other side. Is that where Webster is hiding? I heft the gun in one hand and reach for the handle with the other—but the banging comes again from the last cell. It's too deep in the shadows for me to make it out, but there is someone—something?—there, a shape in the darkness. My eyes slowly adjust, and my throat constricts.

Victor.

My first feeling, upon recognizing him, is immense relief. At first, I'm grateful to see that he's in one piece; either Webster put him back together or gave him the tools to do it himself. But then horror rushes in as I take in the details. His stump of an arm reaches through the bars toward me. His remaining hand clings to the metal bars, twisting furiously as if trying to snap them, his grip so hard, it strains the stitches on his forearm. His face, pale and sallow. His eyes, like dark pits, no recognition in their depths. His jaws snap, slavering, at the air, as he breathes in my scent. He lets out a low, wordless groan of hunger rumbling deep in his chest.

My stomach lurches. The hunger has taken over. Even if I had the key to open the huge padlock on the cell door, I'd just be walking into the arms of my own death, not the man I came here to save.

"Oh, Victor," I whisper, blinking away tears. I can't get a good look at him, but I can see the wear and tear on his body—the torn stitches, the twisted parts where he must have contorted himself trying to escape. He must be in so much pain. "I... I brought food for you..." I shift closer, still keeping my gun aimed at the door behind me. I reach into my pocket for the beef jerky I brought to tide him over until I get him to the cooler in the car—but my fingers find nothing. My heart plummets. I must have dropped the food in the forest during my confrontation with the creature. "I... It's going to be all right. I'll be right back, I swear, and then we're going to get out of here."

He only snarls, lunging through the bars so fast, I have to jump back. The moment I turn fully toward him, his mismatched eyes shift to something behind me. To my shock, he steps back as well, recoiling, as if *afraid* of something.

I register the creak of a door and then there's a crackle of electricity, and pain shoots through every cell of my being.

* * *

I blink awake, the world lurching. My mouth is dry, and there's a sharp throbbing in the side of my head. Something cold and gritty presses against my cheek. It takes me a moment to realize it's the floor. I'm lying on the floor.

I look up and see a thin silhouette leaning over me. A woman's face, lips curved in a cruel smile that doesn't meet her empty, dark eyes. She's middle-aged, with dark hair cut in a short bob. Her body is slim and whiplike, her skin pale in a way that looks almost sickly, like she hasn't seen the sun in years.

"Ah," she says. "Good. I wasn't sure if that voltage would kill you."

I force myself to sit up despite the throbbing in my skull and reach for my gun, but of course it's gone. The woman tuts, shaking a finger at me. In the other hand, she holds the taser that must have taken me down.

I scramble back away from her instinctively, and her smile only widens. "Careful, now," she says.

Then there's a guttural snarl from behind me. I realize I'm almost against the bars of Victor's cell, and lurch forward onto my hands and knees just as his hand lunges through the bars. He manages to rip a few strands of my hair free before I get away. I press a hand to my mouth to stifle a cry.

"You must be the infamous Lucy," the woman says, still smiling in that unhinged way. "He screamed for you, you know. When he was still capable of forming words, I mean." She tilts her head. "And I suppose you know who I am."

I glower up at her, still on my hands and knees on the floor. My ankle is throbbing in tune with my head; I'm not sure if it can support my weight after all of the abuse today. "A monster."

Instead of denying it, she lets out a quiet, thoughtful *hmm*. "Is one who creates monsters a monster themself?" she asks, a question directed not at me, but seemingly at the air, or herself.

"Victor's not a monster," I spit at her.

"No?" She glances behind me, where I still hear Victor rattling his bars and growling like a rabid animal. "Well, even if you're in denial about him, you didn't seem to harbor such sentiments for my poor second creation, now did you? You made quite the mess of him. Quite impressive, given what a tiny thing you are." She studies me. "I've never made a female creature before. Could be interesting..."

I swallow back a surge of nausea at the thought of being strapped to that table, of her standing over me with a scalpel in hand and a gleam in her eye. "He would've killed me if I didn't kill him."

"Indeed, such is the way of the world." She steps closer. I have an urge to recoil, but that would send me back into Victor, so I have no choice but to remain still as she reaches forward and—strangely, sickeningly—tucks a strand of hair behind my ear. I flinch away as her finger grazes my cheek. "Good bone structure," she notes absently before seeming to regain the thread of the conversation. Her eyes flick up to mine, and she says, "I looked into you, you know, after I heard what happened.

Your taxidermy work is marvelous."

I swallow hard, say nothing. The idea of this woman looking at my creations makes my skin crawl with discomfort.

"But they aren't true creations," she continues. "They lack that spark of life." Her lips curve, her eyes intent on mine. "Would you like to know my secret? I could tell you."

For a moment, I can't manage words. "The secret? The secret to creating life?" She only smiles. "Why would you ever tell me that? Why would you tell me *anything*?"

She shrugs, as if it's of little importance. "You interest me. I've never met a kindred spirit," she says. "I think you and I could do great things together. Terrible, wonderous things."

I have several choice words I'd like to say to that, but I hold my tongue as I glimpse movement out of the corner of my eye. "Things like Victor?" I ask quickly, hoping it will prompt her into talking more rather than turning to notice what I've seen — the hand, crawling across the floor toward us.

Her expression tightens. "Victor is just a beta test," she says. "We could do better. Your work made me think about throwing in animal parts, or..."

I tune out the rest as she begins to ramble. I can't deny that a part of me is tempted by her offer. I *would* like to know the secret to creating life. I picture my taxidermy creations in movement, light filling their glass eyes, and it makes my heart *soar*. I don't even dare to picture my mother, or Ellie, opening their eyes to see me again.

The things I could do if I had that secret — the people I could *save* — if I just went along with it long enough to find out her secret. Even if she killed Victor, I could bring him back. I would never have to worry about losing anybody again. I could open my heart without fear, for once.

But even as I consider what that future would look like, I think of Victor's torment. His hunger. His lack of memories about his previous life. Webster created a new life when she made him, but she did not bring back the old one. It is not the same.

And either way, there is no real choice. Not when Webster's madness and cruelty would forever taint any knowledge I gain from her. When I feel movement crawling up the back of my leg, I don't flinch, and subtly reach behind me. The hand drops something into my palm.

"What makes you think I can't figure out your secret myself?" I ask, trying to gain Webster's attention again. She blinks at me, cutting off her stream of words, and barks a laugh.

"Oh, girl," she says. "You have no idea how much research it took me. How many experiments. You don't have the stomach to get your hands dirty like I did, I can tell. You don't have what it takes to keep a *thing* like Victor in line—"

She cuts off and looks down at her shoes, frowning, to see Victor's detached hand untying the laces of her shoe. "What?" She wrinkles her nose, kicks it off. "Foul little thing. How did you...?" She lifts her eyes to me, and her expression changes. "Ah. Don't tell me *that* was your plan."

"No," I say. "That was the distraction." I slide the key into the lock on Victor's cell and turn it behind my back.

Webster's eyes widen, and she steps back, lifting her baton. "You fool," she says. Then she barks out a laugh, still retreating down the hallway. "All you've done is earn a quick death."

As she turns to run, I turn as well to face Victor as he lunges at me from the shadows.

Chapter Thirty-One

I swallow a scream and dodge to the side as Victor lurches toward me. His teeth snap shut with an audible click as he barely misses my shoulder.

"Victor, *stop*!"

He shows no reaction to my words, not even a flicker of recognition at his name. Though it's the same face, the same body, that I've grown to trust and care about over our time together, when I look in his eyes, I don't see Victor. I see nothing but a bottomless well of hunger.

I knew it would be a gamble, setting him free. But I still trust him more than I could ever trust Webster. I believe he can overcome his hunger.

"Please," I say, retreating down the hallway, hobbled by my injured ankle. I smell smoke; the fire still must be spreading. Webster is surely fleeing this very moment. If I could only get Victor to listen to me for *one* minute, we could get out of here. I'm sure if he regains even a shred of his mind, he'll hunt for Webster instead of me. His revenge is so close, but he's so lost, he doesn't even know it. "I have meat for you in the car, we just need to get there—"

Victor lunges again, snarling. I give up, turning to run with the hope of leading him to the car. I make it three steps, and my abused ankle gives out on me. I crash to the concrete floor with a yelp of pain, and the taste of copper fills my mouth.

Victor is right on my heels, his eyes blank as he reaches for me. I kick out with my good leg, aiming for the weak line of stitches on his right leg. It twists. When he steps forward again, the bottom half of his leg doesn't follow, sending him toppling to the floor. I scramble backward toward that awful operation room and the stairs. The closer I get, the more smoke fills the air, making my eyes water and my throat constrict. *The fire.* It's getting closer by the second.

Heedless of the smoke, Victor crawls after me on all fours, like an animal. His pupils are huge, his expression dark and animalistic and locked on the trickle of blood from where I bit my lip. His nostrils flare, and when he breathes in, I know he's scenting me. Scenting prey. Scenting *meat.*

Something crawls over my stomach; I nearly shriek before I realize it's the detached hand. It's carrying a scalpel, which it waves insistently up at me. My breath hitches. Does it want me to use it *against* Victor? Some last piece of his psyche turning against his body's instincts? I grab the scalpel and clutch it in my sweaty palm, but the thought of using it on Victor makes me ill.

"Victor," I say, my voice trembling. "You know who I am. You're not going to hurt me."

My back hits a wall. In the second it takes me to glance to the side to find the door leading out, Victor is on me.

I shut my eyes and thrust out a hand to defend myself.

My bare palm lands on Victor's chest—and to my surprise, it stops him, his teeth snapping shut inches away from my face. He pauses, something flickering across his expression as he glances down at my trembling hand. He must feel my warmth even in this state. It's enough to spark a weak hope within me. My other hand, still clutching the scalpel, stays in my lap.

"Look at me," I whisper. "Please, Victor."

His eyes lift to mine. For a moment, his blank stare makes me fear the worst, but then he blinks, and recognition fills his face, transforming him back into the man I know.

"Lucy," he says, in a hoarse, raw voice. He wrenches himself back away from me and stumbles to his feet. His fingers twist into his own hair, yanking at it. "Oh, God, Lucy. You can't be here. I can't... I can't control..."

"You can." I force myself to hold my chin high even as I tremble. I try to tune out the smoke thickening in the air, and the thought of Webster, and everything except the man in front of me. The man I trust. "You're stronger than this. I know you are. You're not the monster she thinks you are."

"But I am," he whispers. "I am the monster she made me."

"You're not!" I don't trust my ankle, but I scoot forward on my hands and knees, reaching a hand toward him. Now he's the one who retreats, stumbling backward as if he's scared of *me*.

"Stay away from me," he growls in warning. "It's not safe, Lucy. I'm not safe! The way you smell..." He groans, a raw, pained sound. His eyes flit around, frantic, and land on the scalpel in my hand. "Give me that," he says. The hand reaches for it, too, but I snatch it back.

"No," I say, seeing his intent. He'll hurt himself rather than hurt me, but I can't accept that. "Listen to me, Victor. Webster is *right upstairs.* Fleeing as we speak."

"Webster," he whispers, like he's just remembered her existence.

"That's right. Webster. The woman you came so far to kill. Your chance is here, Victor. All you have to do is walk away. Go after her instead of me."

He stares at me for a second, and then his eyes go to the door behind me. "Webster," he says again, and his features twist. I can see that feral look in his eyes again as the hunger takes over, hopefully with a new target. "Hungry…"

"Webster," I remind him.

He lurches forward a step, and then another, like he's sleepwalking. I curl into the corner and try to make myself as small of a target as possible. The hand crouches on my lap like it's ready to fight the rest of its body all by itself. But Victor stumbles past me, into the doorway, and I breathe a sigh of relief.

But then he stops. "No," he says. "Lucy."

When he looks down at me, a chill runs down my spine, and I brace myself—until I look into his eyes and see *him*. Not the hunger, but Victor.

"What?" I ask, dumbfounded. "Victor, you don't have time, she already has a head start."

He shakes his head. "I'm not leaving you."

"I'm fine," I insist, pushing myself to my feet. Or *foot*, rather, as when I put weight on the second leg, I have to bite back a cry of pain. I lean against the wall, struggling to stay upright. "I'll be fine. Victor, you have to go. She's going to get away."

Truthfully, I'm terrified at the prospect of hobbling out of here alone. It isn't that far, but the fire seems hotter and closer by the second as it eats away at the building around us.

This place could collapse… I could end up trapped by debris… There are so many things that could go wrong. But I can't ask Victor to stay with me. Not when he's so close to the thing he's chased all of this while. I hobble forward determinedly, my eyes on the staircase, unable to look at Victor in case he'll see how scared I am.

But a moment later, strong arms close around my waist and lift me up.

"Victor? What are you—"

"I'm not leaving you here." He shifts my weight easily, cradling me against his chest. I feel it rise as he breathes in and see the tremble that goes through him at my scent—but he tightens his grip on me and holds me closer.

"I can walk," I insist. "Webster—"

"Shut up about Webster," Victor whispers. "You're more important."

The simple words make tears rush to my eyes. I press my face into Victor's chest so he won't see how emotional I am as he carries me through the operation room. He pauses there, looking at the scattered pages of notes she abandoned in her haste.

"I heard your conversation with her," Victor says. "If you want to grab some of this—"

"No," I say. As much as a part of me is tempted by it, I don't want to benefit from the cruel work of that woman. "I don't need anything from her."

No matter what her delusions of grandeur tell her, she didn't find a secret to returning someone to life—because as much as I love him, I know that Victor is not the man he was before he died. He's someone wonderful, but he's someone else.

The secret of who he was once likely lies in these scattered pages as well. But when I look up at Victor, I see him reaching the same conclusion as I have.

We need nothing from the monster who made him. We will

build our own future, and we will do better than she did.

"Let her legacy burn," I whisper. Victor nods and ascends the staircase, clutching me tighter. Despite the flames, I have never felt as safe as I do in his arms.

Chapter Thirty-Two

"I must've passed out after that," I say, sitting with my hands folded neatly in my lap. "And when I woke up, I was alone in a hotel room. He was gone."

It's obvious, from the look on Dr. Wright's face, that she doesn't believe me. But I don't think I need her to. I just need to spin a convincing enough story for her to let this go. I hope I've done that by giving as much of the truth as I dare to give.

She glances at Director Ramsey, who is studying me with an unreadable expression. Though honestly, his expression is never readable to me. There's something strange about him, like he's always wearing a mask.

That thought reminds me of something Victor mentioned in passing—*that thing pretending to be Director Ramsey*—and I clench my hands hard to suppress a shiver.

"Do you believe he is dangerous?" Ramsey asks.

"No," I say. I'm not able to meet his eyes, but I try to reassure myself that whoever—whatever—he is, he seems to be perfectly cooperative with Dr. Wright, who I trust to a certain extent. "In all our time together, despite his threats and ample opportunity, he never harmed me or anyone else." I put on my best innocent face. "He even let Webster go, in the end."

Ramsey sits back in his chair and nods up at Dr. Wright.

"Well, in that case, we'll keep an eye out for him. Please let us know if he makes any attempt to contact or threaten you," she says. "But we're not going to turn it into a full-scale manhunt. The MRF has more pressing issues." She pauses, as if deciding whether or not she wants to say something, before adding quietly, "X-14 suffered gravely under these walls. We let him down for a very long time, and there's no excuse for it. So long as he's not a danger, I'm not in any haste to drag him back." Her eyes stay on mine, her look pointed. *She knows.* I hold her gaze and dip my chin in a tiny nod.

"As for you, Ms. Sullivan," Dr. Wright says, shifting back to crisp professionalism. "Obviously, I cannot apologize enough for what you've experienced. We're already making moves to address the security errors and lack of proper staffing that made this possible."

I nod and say nothing. We both know that I could seek legal representation and bring down hell on the MRF for what happened to me...but also that I don't want to. It would only draw unwanted attention both to Victor and this place. Despite its flaws, I do believe that Dr. Wright is trying to do good work here, and I have no intention of ruining that.

I was prepared to use legal action as a threat if I needed to, but as our eyes meet, I think Dr. Wright and I have an unspoken understanding already.

She clears her throat. "We don't have any other subjects at the moment that require your full attention, but there's always a need for someone with your talents on staff."

"I would love to continue working here," I say. Maybe it would be safer to extricate myself from this place, but I can't deny that it excites me, thinking about working with more of the facility's monsters. Learning what I can about the unknown. "But..."

"Ah." Dr. Wright smiles slightly, leaning back in her chair. "I figured there was a but coming."

"I want to go back to school," I say. "I've realized it's important to me. I'd like to finish my degree and become a doctor, officially. I'm tired of having to correct people. And..." I look down into my lap. "I realize I was running away from something I should've faced head-on the first time. This will let me better serve my future patients."

"I can respect that," Dr. Wright says. "And I'm sure the MRF would be happy to have you back as soon as your degree is complete, if that's something you're interested in."

"It is." I smile. "You're welcome to reach out to me for any emergencies in the meantime, and I'll help when I can. As it so happens, I've fallen in love with the area. I purchased a house just to the west of Ash Valley, as a matter of fact, and I plan to move here as soon as I'm done with my studies."

Dr. Wright's eyebrows shoot up. "That's excellent news. Though...to the west?" She frowns. "There's nothing much out that way, is there?"

"Exactly," I say, with a flicker of a smile. "I'll have privacy, just the way I prefer it."

"I see." Again, I suspect from the shrewd look in Dr. Wright's eyes that she sees quite a bit more than that. When I stand, she does as well, and extends a hand to shake. "I look forward to working with you, future Dr. Sullivan."

I smile at her. "Same to you, Dr. Wright."

"There's one more thing..." Her brow creases, and my smile fades. "I'm surprised you didn't ask about Dr. Webster."

I blink. "Have you found any information about her?"

CHAPTER THIRTY-TWO

"No. She seems to have disappeared. We've had no contact."

I force a casual shrug. "I doubt you will," I say. "Given that she knows Victor and I escaped her clutches, I doubt you'll ever hear from her again." My smile returns. "And I think that's for the best."

Dr. Wright nods. "I see. Well, I hope you're right. I must mention that neither Director Ramsey nor I ever reached out to Dr. Webster about X-14's escape. I suspect she was keeping tabs on him another way. Perhaps a tracking device, or an information leak within the facility. It's possible she will come looking for him, or for you."

"I appreciate the warning," I say. "But as I said... I doubt we have to worry about her."

* * *

Mara is waiting for me outside of Dr. Wright's office. The moment I emerge, she throws her arms around my neck in a tight embrace—and after a slight hesitation, I hug her back. I can't remember the last time I had a hug. Or anyone who would want to hug me. It feels rather...nice.

"I was so glad to hear you're okay," she says, pulling back and searching my face. "You *are* okay, right?"

"I'm fine." I smile, touched by the concern. "Thank you for sending Somnus to check in on me. I *did* tell him I wasn't in any real danger."

"Yeah, he told me, but...it was hard not to worry once he couldn't visit your dreams anymore."

I squeeze her arm and then walk with her toward my office to collect my things. "I'm sorry to concern you. But really, Victor never had any intent of harming me."

She shoots me a mischievous sideways glance. "Still 'Victor,' then, huh?"

I bite my lip, shake my head, and refuse to comment.

She giggles. "Fine, keep your secrets."

Mara helps me pack up the scant personal items from my office and walks me to the front lobby. "This is such a shame," she says. "I thought you'd be a great asset for the MRF. And...I dunno...maybe even a friend."

I can't stop a shy smile from creeping across my face. "I'll be back," I promise. "Even before I graduate, I intend to visit. I bought a house out here."

"Really?" She brightens. "Oh, *please* let me know when you're in town. I have a feeling we have a lot to talk about."

I can't help but grin back at her. I've never been very good at making or keeping friends, but I like Mara. I do. Maybe it's time to give the whole idea of socializing another try. "I suspect you're right," I tell her. I pause to brush hair out of my face and give her a sly look. "Perhaps we could even have a double date sometime."

Her eyes widen slightly, and then she returns my smirk. "Oh, now *that* would be interesting."

We hug goodbye, and I walk away knowing that we'll see each other again. Perhaps one day, I'll even tell her the full story. Something tells me she'll understand better than most.

Chapter Thirty-Three

The house is quiet and dark when I walk in. I pause in the entryway to flick on a light.

It's still hard to believe this house is mine. *Ours.* It's a shame I won't be able to live here full-time until after I finish school, but there is something comforting about knowing that I'll always have a home to return to. And by that, I don't only mean the house.

Victor will be traveling while I'm away at school, seeing more of the world he's been denied for so long. But this place will always be waiting. A safe haven for both of us.

"Hello?" I call. There's no response other than a faint scuttling sound from the other room. I slip off my shoes and walk deeper inside. My taxidermy creations peer at me from the walls, watching over me as always. The house isn't furnished yet, but it has beautiful bones. So much space to fill. I know together, we'll build something wonderful here. "Are we playing games again?"

I enter the kitchen and see Victor's detached hand sitting on the countertop with a slip of paper clutched in its fingers.

I lift an eyebrow. "Where is the rest of you?"

It waves the paper at me.

I sigh and pluck the paper from its fingers. I give the hand an affectionate pat before unfolding it; Victor and I still haven't reached a consensus on whether or not it's still a part of him or a being of its own, but either way, he's stuck with his decision not to have the hand reattached.

I glance at Victor's messy handwriting on the paper: *COME TO THE BASEMENT.*

"You and your games," I mutter, smiling despite myself. I reach up to let my hair out of its ponytail and shake it out before heading to the basement door.

I love the remote mountain location, but the main thing that really pulled me to this house was the basement. It's a rarity in Arizona. I believe the original owner was some kind of survivalist nut who wanted a bomb shelter, but I have a more practical use in mind.

I shut the door behind me and descend the creaky steps into the darkness, letting the suspense build before I pull the string on the light bulb overhead. The basement is mostly bare concrete, with a rough wooden counter along one wall, currently occupied by my notes and a variety of medical tools. We've only purchased one other piece of furniture for the room so far: a metal table.

Victor is stretched out on it, his shirt half unbuttoned to expose a sliver of muscular green chest bisected by a thick scar. He turns his head to look at me and offers a cheeky grin.

I place a hand on my hip. "Here for your checkup?"

He bites his lip. "Yes, ma'am."

"Hm..." I walk over to the counter and grab a scalpel, dragging the end of it across the wood as I regard Victor. "Take off your clothes."

"That's not usually part of a checkup—"

"Victor." I point the scalpel at him. "Now."

He grins and lifts himself up on his elbows as he unbuttons his shirt. He tosses it to the floor, and then undoes his pants as well. His hand lingers, fondling the obvious bulge through his briefs, before he discards that last material and leaves himself fully, gloriously naked. I let my eyes drag over his perfect scarred body, drinking in the taut muscles and lines of stitching that make up the man I've fallen for. My gaze wanders all the way down his body, and then shifts up to that beautiful, pierced, very hard cock.

"That's quite inappropriate," I breathe.

"It's always like that."

I roll my eyes and reach down to slide my panties down beneath my skirt. I leave them on the floor and keep the rest on as I approach the table and press the flat of the scalpel to his cheekbone, just above where his teeth show through.

"Lie back," I murmur. "Let me get a good look at you."

He eases onto his back on the table, his eyes locked on me and his pupils very wide and dark. I slowly trace the scalpel down the side of his neck and across his collarbone, lovingly pressing it into the scar above his non-beating heart. I slide the metal across his chiseled abdomen and pause as I reach the base of his shaft. He's as hard as a rock, and already leaking a bit of precum. I swipe it up with a finger of my free hand and suck it into my mouth.

"Fuck," he groans. "Please get up here and ride me. *Please.*"

I smirk. "Well, only because you asked so nicely."

I climb on the table and straddle his hips. Victor gazes up at me with something like awe as I press the edge of the scalpel to his neck. I'm careful not to cut him while I drag my core up and down the outside of his shaft without letting him inside of me, spreading my slickness over his length. Victor groans and reaches up to grab my hip. I push it away with my free hand, pinning it to the table beside his head.

"Keep this up and I'll have to buy some restraints for this table after all," I murmur.

He grins. "Promise?"

I lean down to kiss the smirk off his face, and finally let myself sink down onto his hard length, inch by inch. Every time, he stretches me out so deliciously. I ride him slowly, coaxing pleasure from both of our bodies with each roll of my hips. He feels so fucking good inside of me, like he was made just for me. I toss the scalpel aside before I forget I'm gripping it and sit up to find a better angle, throwing my head back and moaning.

"God, Lucy," he groans, staring up at me. "You're perfect."

Still grinding on him, I run one finger along the row of stitches over his chest, then splay my fingers over the place where his heart is. "So are you."

I roll my hips faster, bouncing on top of him, and there's no more talking. Just my small sounds of pleasure, and his fingers digging bruises into my skin, and his hips jerking up to meet mine.

We come at the same time, our eyes locked. But I barely have time to sink down against his chest before he scoops me up and takes me over to the counter. He pushes into me again, and I welcome him eagerly.

* * *

Afterward, I curl up on his lap as he leans against the wall, both of us sweaty and exhausted. I reach up to run my fingers through his hair, and he leans into my touch, his eyes shut.

"Did you enjoy that?" I murmur.

"Very much." He smiles without opening his eyes.

I wasn't so sure, at first, when he suggested this kind of roleplay, given all that he's been through. It's clear he's into it, but I always make sure to check in afterward.

"And you?" he asks, opening his eyes to gaze down at me.

I flush. "If the several orgasms weren't indicative enough... yes. A lot."

"Good." He grabs my wrist, brings my hand to his lips, and kisses my palm. "I figured we should get some good use out of that table before you sully it with your experiments."

I sigh. "Yes. I suppose we can't keep the body in the deep freezer forever."

We both pause, thinking of all of the pieces of Webster, carefully wrapped and stored. As I told Dr. Wright, we don't have to worry about her bothering us anymore. As I *didn't* tell Dr. Wright, we stumbled upon her after leaving the flaming laboratory. She would've escaped, had she not been trying to drag a safe with her to her car.

I'm grateful for her greed. Because not only did Victor get his revenge, but that safe funded this house for us.

There was a notebook in the safe as well, a small black book that radiated malice. I fed it to the fire while Victor tore Webster to pieces behind me.

But the money felt like something we deserved. And it was hard to turn down such a readily available food source for Victor until we find out a better solution to deal with his cravings. Plus, I've been thinking of using a few pieces of her to start running some experiments.

"Well, we could," I correct myself, shrugging. "But it would be a waste of a perfectly good corpse."

Victor grins at me. "We can't have that."

"Though like I've said, if you're uncomfortable with me using her body..."

"No." He lifts my hand to his mouth again, playfully nipping at my fingers, as if we're having normal pillow talk rather than discussing what to do with a corpse. "We lost all of her research, so she might as well contribute to science in a different way."

"Good point." I questioned my judgment when I realized I was going to have to start from scratch on Webster's work. It's possible her notes would've held information that could help make Victor's life easier—subduing the hunger, or other secrets. But I've always been a person who prefers to do my own work.

Noticing the distance in my eyes, Victor pulls me closer against his chest and kisses my forehead. "You'll figure it out," he whispers. "Fuck Webster. You're smarter than she ever was. You know more about me than she ever did. And the rest, you'll learn."

I lean against him with a happy sigh. "I'd be happy to spend the rest of my life figuring you out."

And I still may never understand him, I know that now. The impossibility of his body and his existence may always be a mystery to me—but I've been able to accept that. I don't need to understand everything about him to trust him.

Or to love him.

I feel him smile against my skin, and I know, even though neither of us have said the words, that he feels the same. "Good. Because I'm all yours, Lucy. Every piece of me is yours."

As we sit quietly, I feel at peace, knowing that all of our broken edges fit perfectly together.

Acknowledgments

Last year, I dove into self-publishing with The Nightmare's Kiss full of nerves and excitement. I had no idea what to expect. Since then, I've been blown away by the enthusiasm and support of my readers and the indie romance community.

So, first of all, to everyone who has read, reviewed, and otherwise shown love for me and my weird little books: thank you, thank you, thank you. Seriously, every time I hear from someone who enjoyed reading my work, it makes my day. I appreciate you all so much!

I would also like to thank:

The endlessly brilliant Impyeu, who once again knocked it out of the park with this cover. (Check her out on Instagram, @1mpyeu!)

Developmental editor Sarah Chorn, who has such a talent for bringing out the best in stories.

Copyeditor Claudette Cruz ("The Editing Sweetheart"), the slayer of typos and continuity errors.

My beta readers L&N, Kristen, and Jenny, for giving excellent advice on messy early drafts of this story.

The Romance Author's Writing Group and Indie Authors Ascending on Discord, for always giving great advice and making this writing life a little less lonely.

And lastly, my family, partner, and friends who have continued to support me along this wild journey. Sorry to those of you who learned some things about me that cannot be unlearned, and you're welcome to those who discovered the delights of monsterfuckery.

About the Author

Skyla Gray is a romance author fond of all things scary and steamy. When not writing, she can usually be found gaming, cooking, or binge-watching horror movies. She lives in Arizona with her partner and an absolute rascal of a dog.

Sign up for my newsletter for an extra spicy bonus content!

You can connect with me on:

🌐 http://skyla-gray.com

🔗 https://www.instagram.com/skyla.gray.romance

Subscribe to my newsletter:

✉ https://skyla-gray.ck.page/e838b44108

9 798989 439812